Creature Catchers

Lisa Smedman

annick press
toronto + new york + vancouver

Annick Press Ltd.

We acknowledge the support of the Canada Council for the Arts, the Ontario Arts Council, the Government of Canada through the Book Publishing Industry Development Program (BPIDP) and the Ontario Book Publishing Tax Credit (OBPTC) for our publishing activities.

Edited by Pam Robertson
Copy edited and proofread by Elizabeth McLean
Interior design by Vancouver Desktop Publishing Centre
Cover design by Roberta Batchelor
Cover illustration by Alisa Baldwin

Cataloging in Publication

Smedman, Lisa
    Creature catchers / by Lisa Smedman.

ISBN-13: 978-1-55451-058-0 (bound)
ISBN-13: 978-1-55451-057-3 (pbk.)
ISBN-10: 1-55451-058-9 (bound)
ISBN-10: 1-55451-057-0 (pbk.)

    I. Title.

PS8587.M485C74 2007   jC813'.54   C2006-904426-0

Published in the U.S.A. by Annick Press (U.S.) Ltd.

Distributed in Canada by	**Distributed in the U.S.A. by**
Firefly Books Ltd.	Firefly Books (U.S.) Inc.
66 Leek Crescent	P.O. Box 1338
Richmond Hill, ON	Ellicott Station
L4B 1H1	Buffalo, NY 14205

Printed and bound in Canada

Visit our website at www.annickpress.com

*For Kyle, who loves creatures
of all shapes and sizes,
real and imaginary.
A world of discovery awaits you.*

Acknowledgments

Thanks once again to the members of my writer's group for their careful critiquing, and to the editors at Annick Press.

1

Kenneth glanced around. No one was looking. His twin sister, Candace, was roller skating in circles over by the unicorn pen, her curly blonde hair fluttering out behind her. Near her, a zookeeper was busy pitchforking flowers into the pen. Uncle Nigel had gone to buy a packet of charcoal to feed to the fire salamanders.

Thanks to the commotion Candace was making, the metal wheels of her skates clattering on the cobblestones, none of the people strolling along the zoo's winding paths on this bright summer day would notice Kenneth scraping. That was perfect, since he didn't want to get caught. He flicked open the pocketknife he'd gotten for his eleventh birthday and scratched at the black paint that covered the front window of the exhibit. Slowly, the glass behind it was exposed.

Their uncle had brought them to the Londinium Zoo to see some of the creatures he'd captured for the 1893 World Exposition in Chicago. The creatures were temporarily on display here, in the zoo's exotics section, before being shipped out next week. Uncle Nigel had shown them a hippogriff, and a Japanese kirin, and an African intulo—something that looked half man, half lizard—but what Kenneth *really* wanted to see was the cockatrice.

He'd viewed a zoetrope of it, of course, but looking through the slits of a spinning cylinder at painted pictures wasn't Kenneth's idea of excitement. The cockatrice sounded savage—something like a fighting cock, except with lizard scales instead of feathers, a long forked tongue, and an enormous hooked claw on the tip of each of its leathery wings. Uncle Nigel had described its eyes as "green as demon ichor and equally venomous."

There were only a handful of people in the world who had looked upon one of these fierce animals and lived. One glance from their eyes, and a person would be petrified—frozen stiff! Just wait until the boys at school heard that Kenneth had actually seen one. *That* would shut them up. Surely they'd stop teasing him about being so short and listen to him, for a change.

The hole was big enough now. He glanced around—no one was looking—and squatted next to the glass, ready to peer inside.

Her arms held out like wings, Candace did a wobbly turn on the roller skates she'd gotten for her birthday. She imagined herself on the back of a pegasus, taking a graceful soar above the beautiful flower gardens below. Some day, in the Lady Candace Owen's Public Gardens, there would be a stable filled with pegasi and unicorns, and sea-foam steeds, and all manner of beautiful horses. Rides would be free for the children who lived in the Poor House. It was just a dream, of course, but one day that dream would come true.

Skating to a halt at the unicorn pen, she leaned on the wooden rail and stared at the magnificent beast. The unicorn was white as an Arabian steed, but small, like a pony, with a spiral horn and crystal hooves that flashed like diamonds in the sun. It looked at her with soft round eyes while munching on the flowers the zookeeper had provided.

Candace leaned over the rail and extended a hand. The unicorn lifted its head, then took a step toward her. Its breath whuffled softly against her palm as it nuzzled her hand.

"I wish I had an apple for you, dear heart," she told it.

The unicorn snorted and tossed its long white mane.

"Here now!" the zookeeper admonished. "Get your hand out of there, Miss. That beast bites."

Candace did as she was told, though knew that she needn't have bothered. The unicorn wasn't about to bite her; it knew she was its friend. Every animal she'd ever met trusted her. She could even get Mrs. Soames's mean little dog to lick her hand—something Kenneth could never hope to do.

She would have loved to inform the zookeeper that there was no danger—that the unicorn would just nuzzle her hand—but she didn't. Correcting an adult just wasn't proper, even if the adult in question was a rough-looking man with rolled-up sleeves and unkempt hair. She gave him a smile instead, then turned sharply and skated away.

Straight into a man who was taking a photograph.

His tripod toppled, sending the camera crashing onto the cobblestones, where it smashed into pieces. The photographic plate flew out of the back of it and shattered with a loud crash.

Candace, tangled together with the man in a most undignified pose, heard a sharp whinny, then the thudding of hooves. She glanced up and saw the unicorn bolting away across its pen. With a splintering thud, its horn slammed into the far rail. The unicorn pawed the earth and tried to pull free, but couldn't.

"Hey there!" the zookeeper shouted angrily, dropping his pitchfork. He leaped over the rail and into the pen.

"I apologize, sir," Candace said to the photographer in her sweetest voice as she scrambled to get up. But inside, she was seething. What had the man been *thinking*, setting up his camera immediately behind her? "That was terribly clumsy of me."

The photographer—a clean-shaven man whose collar had come unbuttoned in the fall—clambered to his feet, a furious expression on his face. "That camera," he gritted, "cost five pounds. You've just cost the *Times* a great deal of money and ruined the photograph for tomorrow's advertisement of the contest."

Candace nodded, but she was barely listening. The zookeeper was having difficulties. He'd grabbed the unicorn's horn with both hands and braced a foot on the rail. Although he pulled until his face went red, he couldn't free the beast. The unicorn whinnied in fear and nipped the zookeeper's sleeve, tearing it. By now, a handful of people had stopped to stare.

"Excuse me," Candace said to the photographer. "I'm needed."

Hiking up her skirt, she climbed over the rail and into the pen. The wheels of her skates caught in the dirt, nearly tripping her.

"Oh, Zookeeper!" she called as she staggered across the pen. "If a maiden strokes the unicorn's neck and whispers softly in its ear, it will be calmed."

The zookeeper took one look in her direction as she reached to touch the unicorn, then swore. "Get out of here!"

The unicorn responded to the man's tone by lashing backward with a hoof. Candace dodged it, lost her balance, and fell to her knees. Something soft and squishy seeped through her stocking. It felt like warm oatmeal, and smelled even worse.

Abandoning his attempts to pull the unicorn free, the zookeeper grasped Candace firmly under the arms and lifted her over the rail. Candace landed unsteadily on her skates and turned just in time to see the unicorn yank its horn free. It gave the zookeeper a baleful look and lowered its head, ready to attack.

"No, don't! He didn't mean any harm," Candace

cried to the unicorn, waving her hands to shoo it back.

"Of course not," the zookeeper said, thinking she was talking to him. "But he's dangerous just the same."

"Watch out!" Candace cried as the unicorn lunged forward, but the zookeeper didn't pay her any heed.

The zookeeper yelled in surprise as the unicorn's horn jabbed into his leg, tearing the fabric of his rough gray trousers. As he yelped and slapped a hand over his scratched leg, the unicorn trotted off, a piece of gray cloth hanging from its horn like a flag.

Kenneth heard the sound of breaking glass behind him. Glancing over his shoulder, he saw his sister sprawled atop a small man with wispy blond hair. A broken camera and tripod lay nearby.

Kenneth grinned. Candace was going to get in trouble for that. Best of all, nobody was paying the slightest attention to him.

He pulled a small mirror out of his pocket and held it next to the hole, using it to peer into the cockatrice enclosure. If he only looked at the cockatrice through the mirror, and not directly, he'd be safe. All he could see, however, was some straw. The enclosure looked empty. Perhaps the cockatrice was in a corner. Kenneth lowered the mirror, hesitated. If the cockatrice was near the wall and he took just a quick look, just long enough to catch a glimpse of tail feathers, he'd probably be safe enough. If he backed down now, he'd have nothing to tell the older boys. He took a deep breath, screwing up his courage, and pressed his cheek to the glass, looking directly into the enclosure.

A face loomed into view. A human face: a young man wearing dark goggles that hid his eyes. A tiny mirror was attached, at an angle, to either side of the goggles. The man stared back at Kenneth and made angry "go away" gestures with his hands. Then his palm slapped over the hole from inside.

"Hell!" Kenneth swore.

"Is hotter than a fire salamander's buttocks, so they say," a voice behind him said.

Kenneth spun around and saw Uncle Nigel staring down at him. He held a cone of newspaper smudged with charcoal dust in one hand, his walking stick in the other. His derby was low over his eyes, shading his frown. He was a large man, taller than most, with a thick black mustache that covered his upper lip; he wore it bushy, not waxed. A white line creased his left cheek and the side of his chin. It looked like a dueling scar, but had been caused by a Zulu spear.

Uncle Nigel tapped the silver tip of his walking stick against the hole Kenneth had scratched in the paint. "Trying for a look at the cockatrice, were you?"

Kenneth swallowed nervously. Uncle Nigel was a commanding presence. He could stare down a Malay warrior or a fierce Gurkha, if he had a mind to.

Kenneth glanced at the unicorn pen. Candace was inside it, talking to a man who was trying to pull the unicorn's horn out of the rail. She had manure caked on her button boots, and the hem of her dress had soggy brown stains. Nurse would be furious to see her in such a state. Kenneth pointed at his sister. "Candace—"

"Is not in danger of being petrified," Uncle Nigel said firmly. "You are."

"I wouldn't have been petrified," he told his uncle. "I was using this mirror. See?" A flash of sunlight reflected off the mirror as he held it up for his uncle to see.

For a moment, Uncle Nigel looked impressed. Then his frown returned. "When I saw you, just now, you weren't—"

A shout from the unicorn pen interrupted whatever Uncle Nigel had been about to say. The man who had been in the pen with Candace swore an oath that made several of the women near him blush and hurry away. He shook his fist at the unicorn, then clambered stiffly over the rail. One hand holding his torn trouser leg together, he gave Candace a furious glare, then stomped off.

Uncle Nigel's mouth quirked in a smile.

Kenneth started to glance back at the hole, but Uncle Nigel's sun-browned hand slapped against the glass. He'd dropped the packet of charcoal; the black lumps lay scattered around his feet. "Were you not *listening*, Kenneth, when I told you this creature is dangerous?" he admonished.

Candace clattered up behind Uncle Nigel, manure flying in clumps from the wheels of her skates. Straw was stuck to her black stockings. She smelled like a stable. Her blue eyes shone when she saw Kenneth squirming under Uncle Nigel's fierce glare. There was nothing she liked better than seeing her twin brother get into trouble, especially when she'd just been up to mischief herself. Behind her, the photographer grumbled as he picked up the remains of his camera.

Uncle Nigel rapped his stick against the glass. "Horace," he called out. "It's Nigel. Bring out one of the rabbits, won't you?"

A door opened in the side of the cockatrice enclosure. Out stepped the man Kenneth had seen. He pushed his goggles up onto his forehead. There was a rabbit in his other hand. He held it by one leg.

"Oh!" Candace exclaimed. "Poor little rabbit. You're hurting it!"

"This rabbit don't feel nothing no more," Horace said. He rapped his knuckles against it. "Hard as wood, he is. Petrified." He lowered the rabbit. "Just as well. That way he won't feel nothing when the cockatrice has him for supper."

Candace's face was pale. She looked as if she was going to be sick.

Kenneth glanced up at Uncle Nigel.

Uncle Nigel nodded. "The cockatrice can sense when someone is looking at it," he said. "Quick as a flash, it will turn around, and then it's all over. One glance from its eyes would be all it would take for a lad your size. A grown man might survive, but would suffer partial petrification that would make a ruin of his body.

I met a man in Rome, years ago, who suffered that fate. His lower limbs had stopped working. The poor wretch was reduced to dragging himself around the streets on a wheeled board."

Kenneth knew he was supposed to feel frightened. Horrified, even. He didn't. Instead he was thinking about how amazing it would be to be able to petrify someone with a glance. That yappy dog that Mrs. Soames owned, for example. The next time it tried to bite Kenneth, he could stop it in its tracks.

"It isn't right," Candace said. "It's cruel." Kenneth could see that she was blinking furiously, trying not to cry as she stared at the stone-stiff rabbit. She wouldn't eat rabbit; she hadn't touched it since the day she'd seen their groomsman cutting the head off a hare he'd bagged while hunting. Nor would she eat lamb, or goat, or any other "cuddly" animals. This week, she was even refusing to eat fish.

How kippers qualified as cuddly, Kenneth couldn't say.

"What's the point of collecting a cockatrice if no one ever gets to see it?" Kenneth asked.

Uncle Nigel gave him the look—the one that always came before a lecture. "The cockatrice is on the verge of extinction," he said. "Only a few dozen survive. They must be preserved for future generations to study. That is why the work done by creature catchers is so important."

"I want to become a creature catcher," Kenneth announced.

"You're not old enough," Candace said.

"I'm older than you."

Candace rolled her eyes. "Only by thirteen minutes." Her face grew sly. She skated closer—close enough to loom over him. Even without the skates, she was taller than Kenneth. She never tired of reminding him how small he was.

Kenneth balled his fists. He would never strike a girl, it just wasn't done, but sometimes he was sorely tempted. Surely there was some sort of exception for sisters.

"Children!" Uncle Nigel gently pulled them apart. "You shall both get your chance to collect creatures, soon enough. Tomorrow, the *Londinium Times* will announce a contest for children, sponsored by the Royal Cryptozoological Society. The child who collects the most unusual creature over the next fortnight will receive a copy of the book *A Child's History of England* and will have his or her picture in the newspaper. You can try your hand at capturing a fey moth or a thimble gnome; when I get back from my expedition, I'll show you how to construct a trap."

Kenneth snorted softly to himself. A *thimble gnome*? He couldn't imagine anything less exciting. Every garden in England was chock-a-block with thimble gnomes—fat little worms with vaguely human faces that clung to leaves with their stubby arms and legs. You couldn't even see them properly, except under a magnifying lens. Winning the contest would require a creature that was large and impressive. And fierce.

Uncle Nigel seemed about to say more, but the

photographer stormed up, his tripod under one arm. "Are you the father of this young lady?" he demanded, gesturing at Candace. "My camera—"

"You require compensation," Uncle Nigel interrupted. "Quite right." He reached into his pocket, pulled out a fold of bills, and peeled off a twenty-pound note. "Will this do?"

The photographer's eyes widened. "Yes. Yes, it will indeed. Thank you, sir." He took the bank note, tipped his hat to Uncle Nigel, and hurried away.

Candace had gotten off easily, Kenneth thought as he watched the photographer leave.

Uncle Nigel turned back to Kenneth and Candace. "Let's go see the fire salamanders, shall we?"

Kenneth caught his sister's eye as Uncle Nigel bent to scoop up the charcoal that had spilled. Pretending to be holding a rabbit, he raised the imaginary animal to his mouth and savagely bit its throat.

Candace's face paled.

Kenneth smiled.

Candace leaned over the low stone wall that surrounded the fire salamander pit. She wished Nurse hadn't tied her corset so tight; the whalebones dug into her waist. Kenneth might complain about his scratchy wool stockings and the stiff collar that buttoned onto his shirt, but he had no idea what true misery was. Alas, these were the things a lady had to endure.

She sneaked a hand down to brush the drying mud from her dress. She realized she looked a sorry state, but that was the price you had to pay if you wanted to do some good in this world. A pity the zookeeper hadn't listened to her. He might have avoided that scratch the unicorn gave him.

She tossed some charcoal down to the salamanders below. They were ugly creatures with wrinkled skin that glowed a dull red, eyes that swiveled in different directions, and thick, splayed legs. Each time one gobbled up a lump of charcoal it would let out a belch of flame. From out the other end of the body came what looked like blobs of black, flaming toffee. It smelled like burned broccoli and sulfur.

She'd much rather have stayed to watch the unicorn, but Uncle Nigel said he didn't want to pay for any more broken cameras. So she daydreamed, trying to decide what she would catch for the contest. Fey moths were pretty, with their ever changing, rainbow-colored wings, but every girl in England had at least one of them stuck on a pin in her butterfly collection. To win the contest, she would have to collect something breathtakingly beautiful and inspiring.

Which was exactly what the fire salamanders *weren't*, although Kenneth seemed to find them fascinating. He prattled on to Uncle Nigel about whether a fire salamander would explode if you dropped it into ice water. Candace just wished they would move on. She'd like to visit the aviary and see the fairies flitting about, or the enclosure that held the big cats. The sphinx, she'd heard, had finally awakened from its twelve-year slumber.

Kenneth, however, was asking if they could see the minotaur, a great shaggy bull that walked upright like a man. What a bore that would be! The last time they'd visited its labyrinth, they'd stared down at the maze for an hour without seeing anything.

Candace decided it was time to interrupt. "Tell us about your next expedition, Uncle Nigel," she said. "Where will you be going?"

Uncle Nigel smiled, clearly delighted to be asked about his upcoming trip. "Up north," he said. "To the Moorlands. I intend to collect a will o' the wisp."

Candace and Kenneth both spoke at the same time. "What's a will o' the wisp?"

Uncle Nigel tucked his walking stick under one arm and cupped his hands as if he were holding a tennis ball. "It's about so big," he said. "A creature composed entirely of light."

"It doesn't have a body?" Candace asked.

"No," Uncle Nigel replied. "It's a non-corporeal creature. The latest theory is that it's composed of swamp gas, infused with magic."

Kenneth was also frowning. "If it doesn't have a body, then how will you catch it?"

Their uncle beamed and puffed up his chest as if he'd been hoping for them to ask. "With my latest invention," he said. "An encompassing field of alternating bands of positively and negatively charged

ions that velocitate at a precise—" He saw the confused looks on their faces and paused. "With a big electrical net."

"What color is a will o' the wisp?" Candace asked. She pictured something like the colored light bulbs on the carousel, blinking blue, red, yellow, and green. How pretty that would be in her garden.

"White."

"Oh."

"What does a will o' the wisp do?" Kenneth asked.

"Do?" Uncle Nigel scratched his mustache with the tip of his walking stick. "Why, it just floats around. And . . . glows."

Candace and Kenneth exchanged a look. He was probably thinking the same thing she was. The will o' the wisp sounded boring.

"I read a book on the Moorlands," Candace said. "That's where the pixies have their burrows. They come out at night to dance in circles under the moon. Their voices are like music, it said. They sound like chimes tinkling in the wind. They're terribly shy, but they love cream. You can coax them out and befriend them by leaving out a saucer of cream."

Uncle Nigel raised an eyebrow. "Oh can you, now?"

"Trolls," Kenneth said. "That's what I'd want to catch, if I were going to the Moorlands. They're great, lumbering stupid things, but terribly strong and fierce. But they have a weakness: they turn to stone in sunlight."

Uncle Nigel's other eyebrow rose. "Is that so?"

Kenneth nodded vigorously. "The head boy at my

school said his cousin saw a stone in a field that had been a troll before it—"

"A pixie is what's wanted to win the contest," Candace interrupted.

Kenneth rudely elbowed at her. "No, a troll. Imagine how impressed everyone would be, if you captured a great, huge troll."

"You'd never do it. A pixie, on the other hand—"

"Children, please!" Uncle Nigel held up his hands. "Pixies and trolls are both interesting, in their way, but it's a will o' the wisp I'm after. Nobody's brought back one of those yet." A gleam crept into his eye. "I'll be the first." He leaned closer. "Can you two keep a secret?"

Both Candace and Kenneth nodded eagerly.

"Nobody realizes it yet, but it's the draining of the bogs that releases will o' the wisps. Follow the peat cutters, and you'll find one." He straightened. "Unfortunately, once released into the air, a will o' the wisp doesn't last long. At the rate the Moorland bogs are being drained, there won't be any will o' the wisps left in a year or two."

"Why not stop draining the bogs, then?" Candace asked.

"And do without peat?" Kenneth scoffed.

"What do they need peat for?" Candace asked.

"Their stoves and fireplaces," Uncle Nigel said. "They burn it like we burn coal." He patted Candace on the head. "Not to worry. I'll collect a will o' the wisp before they're gone."

"Are the pixies going to disappear too?" Candace asked. "Shouldn't they be collected as well?"

"Pixies are as thick as mosquitoes in the Moorlands. They're not going to disappear any time soon. And they've already been documented by both Eberts and Higthorn," he added, naming his two chief rivals in the creature collecting business.

"Besides," Kenneth added, "the zoo's already got fairies. Pixies are just more of the same, except uglier. Warty little monsters. They don't even have wings."

"That's not true!" Candace exclaimed. Kenneth didn't know what he was talking about. He didn't even read. Instead he spent all of his time in front of a mirror, practicing his boxing stances. "According to the *Girl's Own Annual,* pixies are beautiful creatures," she continued. "I'd do anything to see one—will you take me with you on your expedition, Uncle Nigel?"

"No, take me!" Kenneth shouted. "I want to see a troll."

"You're both too young to join an expedition."

"But you went to Africa when you were only thirteen!" Kenneth protested.

"And you captured your first creature at fourteen!" Candace added.

Uncle Nigel stroked his mustache, hiding his smile. "That may be, but your parents would never allow it."

Ah, so that was it, Candace thought. Their parents.

"How about this," Uncle Nigel said. "Tomorrow, on my way north, I'll stop by your home and show you my new vehicle. It's a dirigible."

"One of those great sausage-shaped balloons with a basket hanging underneath?" Candace asked.

"Not a basket," Uncle Nigel corrected. "A gondola. Large as a sitting room, and fully enclosed. Windows down both sides, and plenty of cabinets to hold all of my equipment."

Candace stole a look at Kenneth and noted the devious expression on his face. He was probably thinking he could talk Uncle Nigel into taking him. Candace, however, knew this would be a wasted effort. The ones who needed to be convinced were their parents. And Candace knew just how to go about it.

She smiled. The first creature for the Lady Candace Owen's Public Gardens was as good as in the bag. And with it, she would win the contest.

2

Kenneth found his father in the study. Even though it was late afternoon, the curtains were closed. Gloom wrapped itself around the room, casting shadows on the floor-to-ceiling bookshelves and large desk cluttered with papers. Lord Percival Owen was hunched over a book, his spectacles perched precariously on the end of his nose. He squinted against the dim illumination of the gas lamp over his desk. A cup filled with tea sat forgotten on the head of a life-sized statue of a hound that stood next to his chair.

Kenneth had to clear his throat three times before his father finally looked up.

Lord Owen blinked. "Kenneth?"

Kenneth sighed. His father always seemed startled to see him. It was as if Lord Owen sometimes forgot he had children.

"Uncle Nigel's invited me to go for a ride in his dirigible tomorrow," Kenneth began.

Lord Owen nodded absently. Already his gaze was starting to drift back to his book.

"I may be away overnight. I'm going to help him catch a creature."

Lord Owen's expression sharpened. "Off on another ill-conceived adventure, is he?"

"It's not ill-conceived," Kenneth protested. "Uncle Nigel's planned it all out. He's got—"

"No idea what he'll encounter, as usual," his father interrupted.

Kenneth shook his head in frustration. "Yes, he does. He's all prepared. He's got this big electric net that—"

"What's he after this time?" Lord Owen asked. "Something dangerous, no doubt."

"A will o' the wisp." Kenneth cupped his hands. "A little ball of light, about so big. Not dangerous at all."

Lord Owen harumphed. "'Not dangerous?' That's what Shelton said about his cerberus-bulldog cross." He leaned forward, his chair creaking. "If Shelton had stopped to consult a basic mythologica before breeding it, that horrendous incident at the dogfighting ring never would have happened. Any *Tricapitus* species is thrice dangerous. In order to soothe such a beast, each of the heads has to be placated with music of a particular tonal—"

"A will o' the wisp doesn't have three heads," Kenneth pointed out. "I doubt it has any heads at all."

"That's as may be," Lord Owen said, running a hand through his thinning hair. "The point remains that any cryptozoological creature must be properly studied." He turned to the statue beside him. "Take

Canis laelaps, for example." He shifted the teacup to the desk and laid an affectionate hand on the hound statue. "We know that these stone figures were once creatures of flesh and blood, and that they might one day be returned to a living, breathing state. The key to this endeavor lies not in hacking the creature apart with chisel and hammer as Reckett did, but in a careful examination of the original Greek texts." He nodded at the leather-bound book that lay open on his desk.

Kenneth glanced at the dense lines of incomprehensible text, then shook his head. The *laelaps* statue had stood next to his father's desk since Kenneth could remember. If Uncle Nigel had fiddled about for years on end with books and reading, there wouldn't have been any creatures left for him to catch.

Lord Percival's dream was to breed the swiftest hound alive, yet even if he did succeed in turning the *laelaps* back to flesh again and breeding it with a greyhound, Kenneth doubted that his father would even venture out of doors to watch the puppies run. And no matter what his accomplishments, Father would never be as famous or admired as his younger brother.

Uncle Nigel had dash. He'd brought creatures back from darkest Africa, and leaped onto a burning pyre in India to grab a phoenix egg. And he had the scars to show for it. Uncle Nigel was a man of action. And Kenneth's father . . .

Was lost in his book again.

"What about the expedition?" Kenneth asked. "Can I go?"

"I'll speak to your mother about it," his father mumbled.

Kenneth sighed, knowing his father would never get around to it. At best, Father would probably only have a hazy recollection of this conversation.

Which might just work in Kenneth's favor. By the time Nurse discovered that Kenneth was gone and finally got up her courage to interrupt Father's studies, Father might mistakenly think he *had* given Kenneth permission to go with Uncle Nigel.

Kenneth smiled. "Thank you, Father," he said brightly.

His father nodded absently. "Off you go, then," his attention wholly on his reading once more.

Kenneth turned away, leaving him to his books. He could already imagine the look on his father's face when Kenneth returned with his captured creature. Just wait until Father glanced out his study window and saw a *troll* in the back garden.

Hearing the sound of her mother's raised voice inside the drawing room, Candace closed her eyes for a moment in order to brace herself. Lady Millicent Owen was engaged in her favorite pursuit: arguing. Or, as she called it, debating.

"And why *shouldn't* our society demand the vote for creatures, as well as for women?" she said in a strident voice that easily penetrated the thick wooden door.

"It's quite simple, Lady Owen," a male voice replied. "Creatures are not human beings."

"If humanity is the deciding factor, then what of the lycanthrope?" her mother replied. "He is a man twenty-eight days of the lunar month and a wolf for only one day, and yet he is deemed an 'animal' and denied the vote. Where is the logic in that?"

"And if the election should fall on the day that he is a wolf?" the male voice asked with a laugh. "How is he to vote? By raising his paw? Or perhaps by wagging his tail?"

Candace cringed. She could imagine her mother's face heating up, like an iron left too long on the stove. "It is to be universal suffrage, or nothing at all," her mother insisted.

"We include creatures to the detriment of our cause, Lady Owen," a woman's voice interrupted. "If we are to achieve the vote, we must focus on women alone." She paused. "Where will it end, Millicent? Shall we demand the vote for the likes of centaurs?"

"And why *shouldn't* centaurs be included, Agnes?" Candace's mother demanded in a hot voice. "They may have the lower body of a horse, but they're men from the waist up."

"They're indecent!" her visitor protested. Her voice dropped to a hush. "They do their business outside, on the lawn."

The man gave an embarrassed harrumph. "Dear me, is that the time? I should be getting back to the parsonage."

Candace heard the sound of a chair scraping against the floor.

"It's only natural that centaurs should choose to 'do their business' outside, like horses," Candace's mother shot back. "How could a centaur possibly fit inside a room the size of a closet, let alone sit on a toilet?"

Candace heard a rustle of skirts as her mother's second guest abruptly rose to her feet. Then the door opened. Parson Blithe hurried from the room, his walking stick tucked under one arm and his face red. Close on his heels was Lady Agnes Hawthorne, a woman famous for her support of charitable causes. She swept past Candace, her expression grim.

Candace groaned. She had hoped they would be invited to the grand opening of Hawthorne Ladies' College, but her mother had just dashed any chance of that.

Millicent Owen stood in the middle of the drawing room. She refused to wear a corset and thus had a silhouette that resembled a barrel, rather than an hourglass. She had shoved her puffed sleeves up past her elbows and stood with her hands on her hips, like one of the boxers Kenneth so admired. Her expression was one of triumph, as if she'd just bested a foe.

"Lady Hawthorne seemed upset," Candace ventured.

"Some things are more important than people's feelings," her mother replied. Then she gave a heavy sigh. "What is it you wanted?"

"Uncle Nigel's stopping by tomorrow in his dirigible," Candace said brightly. "He invited Kenneth to come creature collecting with him, but said I couldn't come, because I was a girl."

Her mother's face clouded.

"I stood up to him, though," Candace said, hoping she sounded convincing. "I said you would certainly give your permission for me to go."

For a moment, Candace thought her ploy had worked. Her mother actually looked proud of her. Then her mother's mouth set in a firm line. "I won't have it," she said.

Surprised, Candace blurted. "Why ever not?"

"Instead of gadding about catching creatures for zoos, your uncle ought to be supporting our cause," Millicent Owen said in a stern voice.

Candace lifted an eyebrow slightly at the word "our." From what she could see, there was only her mother left in the drawing room.

"He could use one of his lectures to campaign for us," her mother continued, riding her current train of thought at full speed. "But he won't, of course. He cares nothing for the creatures he collects."

"That's not true!" Candace said fiercely. "Uncle Nigel does care. The creatures he collects are going extinct. If he didn't collect them, there'd be none left. They'd all *die*. The zoos—"

"Serve the needs of humans, not the creatures they incarcerate," her mother said. "Why do you think they have bars?"

Candace opened her mouth, then closed it again. Her mother would change her mind about zoos, some day, when she saw the beautiful garden Candace was going to build. The Lady Candace Owen's Public Gardens would be a place of elegance and harmony, where humans could learn to appreciate the pixies' rare beauty and delicate grace. When her mother observed the pixies frolicking in delight in the fountains and blossoms, she'd realize how wrong she'd been to criticize Uncle Nigel and his endeavors.

"What if the creatures wanted to come back with me?" Candace asked. "I could befriend them, and explain that I only want what's best for them, and how well they'd be treated."

"You're not going," her mother said firmly, folding her arms across her chest. "And neither is your brother."

Candace lowered her head. That was it, then. Once her mother's mind was made up, there was no budging her. "Yes, Mother," Candace murmured.

Secretly, however, she was plotting. When Uncle Nigel arrived tomorrow, he was certain to be greeted with a lengthy lecture from Mother on the evils of keeping creatures in zoos. That's when Candace would make her move.

Candace could already picture the look on her mother's face when Mother opened the *Londinium Times* and read about the pixie who had *chosen* to come live in Londinium, at the home of Miss Candace Owen.

Candace smiled. It would be even better than winning the contest.

The dirigible arrived just after dawn. It was, as Candace had guessed, a big sausage that tapered to points at both ends, filled with hydrogen. Electric motors with gigantic wooden propellers hung on either side of the gondola. These whirred as the dirigible descended, nose down, to the lawn.

As it did, a dozen of the groomsmen who had been waiting on the lawn grabbed the ropes that trailed from the dirigible's nose. They pulled it toward a pole that had been erected next to the tennis court, and tied the lead rope to the pole. Other men ran forward with large sacks of sand. They heaved these into the door that had opened in the side of the gondola, weighing the dirigible down so that it would not float away again when Uncle Nigel got off. Slowly, the dirigible settled to the ground.

Kenneth watched from the bushes as Uncle Nigel released a set of stairs and climbed down from the gondola. The dirigible rose slightly as his uncle's foot left the step. The groomsmen added several more sacks as Uncle Nigel strode toward the house.

After that, they stood around talking. One of them pulled out a pipe, but one of the others slapped it out of his hand. Angry words were exchanged as the man who'd done the slapping gestured up at the dirigible and explained that the hydrogen would explode if a spark burned through the fabric of the balloon. The other man retrieved his pipe and stuffed it back in his pocket. Eventually they all moved off, sat down, and began playing cards.

This was Kenneth's chance. He picked up his burlap sack and crept toward the dirigible, keeping behind shrubs as he went along. Several times, the heavy chain inside the sack clanked. Luckily, the men didn't hear it and were too busy with their game to notice him.

He was almost at the gondola when he saw, out of the corner of his eye, someone coming toward the dirigible from the direction of the house. Had Uncle Nigel spotted him? No, it was Candace.

She sprinted the last few steps, elbowing her way past him and taking the gondola stairs in a single leap. Her hair was undone and she was wearing her night-gown under her dress—he could see its frills peeping out from under the hem. She, too, was carrying something: a cloth bag.

Kenneth clambered into the gondola after her.

"What are you doing here?" he hissed.

"The same thing as you," she panted. "Stowing away."

"It was my idea," Kenneth said angrily.

"Nonsense. I thought of it first."

"Nurse will notice you're gone."

"No, she won't," Candace said. "I convinced Mother that I'm unwell: a fainting spell, caused by Nurse forcing me to wear a corset." She put the back of her hand to her head and fluttered her eyelashes dramatically. Her hand dropped. "After shouting at Nurse a bit, Mother sent her out to purchase a tonic for me. It will be mid-morning before she sees the note I left in my room. You, however, will be noticed missing."

"No, I won't," Kenneth said. "I told Nurse I was going fishing. That way, she wouldn't wonder why I was carrying a sack. When I'm late for tea and she starts to worry, *my* note will explain where I've gone."

Candace gave him an approving look. For once, she was willing to admit he'd been clever. "What's inside the sack?" she asked.

"A chain and padlock."

Candace sniffed. "I expect you're going to use that to bind the troll once it's turned to stone?" she said.

Kenneth nodded.

Candace looked smug. "A troll turned to stone will be too heavy for the dirigible. Didn't you feel how it sagged down when you jumped in with your sack? With a great heavy troll on board, it will never get off the ground."

Kenneth hadn't thought of that. He felt his face grow hot. "What's your plan, then?" he asked. "What's in your bag?"

"A bottle of cream," Candace said. "And a saucer."

"That's it?" Kenneth asked. "How do you plan to get the pixies back to the dirigible? Take them by the hand and dance them on board?"

"Don't be ridiculous," Candace snapped. "I'm going to *talk* to them. I'll make friends with them."

Kenneth laughed.

"What?" Candace demanded.

"What if they speak Gaelic, or Welsh?" Kenneth said. "How are you going to talk to them?" He hawked at the back of his throat, as if bringing up phlegm—his imitation of a Welsh accent.

For once, Candace had no reply. She fumed. Suddenly, she glanced out one of the gondola's windows. "Uncle Nigel's coming," she exclaimed. "Hide!"

Together, they scrambled for the cabinets. Kenneth tossed his sack into one that already held a camera and tripod. Candace tucked her bag into another that held hip waders and an oilskin overcoat. Most of the other cabinets were full of Uncle Nigel's equipment. Only one cabinet, at the rear of the gondola, had enough room to hide in. The cabinet had a funny smell, and a large box that made a humming noise on the floor, but it was otherwise empty.

They both crowded in at once, grunting and shoving each other. Somehow, they got the door shut. Kenneth would have liked to push Candace out, but knew that if she were found on board, she'd tell Uncle Nigel about him. They wound up nose to nose in near darkness. Candace stepped on his foot. Kenneth jabbed his finger into her ribs. She stomped on his foot again. Harder.

The dirigible shifted as Uncle Nigel climbed aboard. "A pity about Candace having to miss the dirigible," he was saying—probably to their parents. "I hope she's feeling better soon. And tell Kenneth to save one of the trout he catches for me. We'll fry it up for supper tomorrow when I get back."

From his hiding place in the cabinet, Kenneth heard soft dragging sounds: the ballast sacks being removed. The dirigible rose a little each time. One of the men commented that the gondola didn't have enough lift. More sacks were removed.

Kenneth and Candace exchanged a look as the dirigible's motors whirred to life. Kenneth peeked out through the crack between the cabinet door and its frame. Uncle Nigel stood with his back to the pilot's chair, his hands on his hips. He glanced around the gondola, then down at something on the floor. Kenneth's heart started beating faster as he saw what Uncle Nigel was looking at. Kenneth's boot print.

Instead of inspecting it more closely, however, Uncle Nigel settled into the wicker pilot's chair. A wheel was mounted in a vertical position on the side of the seat, perpendicular to the floor. He rested one hand on top of it and signaled to the men below. They released the ropes and the dirigible moved forward, the motors whirring. Uncle Nigel spun the wheel and the dirigible's nose angled up slightly. He worked the foot pedals and the dirigible slowly turned, then began picking up speed.

Kenneth looked at Candace in the dim light. She looked back at him. Then they both grinned. They'd done it! The nose of the dirigible suddenly tilted even more sharply upward. Kenneth tumbled onto Candace and they banged heads. She elbowed him fiercely. Kenneth stepped on her foot, pretending it was an accident.

The dirigible leveled off again. Kenneth pushed himself away from his sister.

From outside the cabinet came their uncle's voice. "I wouldn't stay in that cabinet," he said. "If you do, the fumes from the battery will make you sick."

Kenneth's hopes of bringing back a troll from the Moorlands sank faster than a sack full of lead.

 **3**

Candace stared up at Uncle Nigel. "You knew we were there all along, didn't you?"

Uncle Nigel's eyes twinkled. "Candace Owen, fainting?" he asked. "Hardly credible. You're made of sterner stuff, my girl." He eyed Kenneth. "And what boy would go fishing when there's a dirigible to be seen? Or stowed away on, eh?"

He paused. "I presume you both left notes for your parents, telling them where you've gone?"

"Of course," Candace and Kenneth said at the same time.

"I wouldn't want Mother and Father to worry," Candace added.

"Or to wonder if I'd hooked a whale and been dragged out to sea," Kenneth said.

Candace rolled her eyes at that one. The stream where Kenneth liked to go fishing was barely knee-deep.

"Good," Uncle Nigel said. "Then let's get on with our journey."

Candace's eyes widened. "You're not going to turn the dirigible around and send us home?"

"How about we just send Candace home, instead?" Kenneth suggested.

Candace scowled at him.

Uncle Nigel laughed. "This will be our little adventure—all three of us—although I expect your mother and father will have a few things to say about it once we get back. Now come up here beside my chair, why don't you, and I'll show you how the dirigible is steered."

Candace and Kenneth both grinned at once—then raced to see who could stand closest to Uncle Nigel's chair. Kenneth won. Candace made a face behind his back, wishing they *had* turned around—to drop Kenneth off.

They listened as Uncle Nigel explained how the foot pedals worked the rudder that turned the dirigible left and right, and how turning the wheel controlled the "pitch"—whether the dirigible's nose pointed up at the sky or down at the ground. He showed them the altimeter, a dial that looked like a clock, except that it had a single hand that pointed to how many hundreds of feet they had climbed.

"Twenty-four hundred feet," Uncle Nigel said. "We've picked up a good tail wind; by my estimation, we're managing about forty knots. We should be over the Moorlands by evening." He shifted over slightly on his chair. "Now, who wants to try their hand at steering?"

"I do!" Kenneth shouted, all but leaping into the chair. He had to stretch so his feet would reach the pedals, but soon was turning the dirigible this way and that in long, slow turns like those of a sailboat changing course. He spun the wheel forward, and a moment later the nose of the dirigible dipped alarmingly.

Uncle Nigel chuckled. "Steady there, lad," he said, easing the wheel back again. "Easy does it."

Candace, meanwhile, had turned her back and was studiously ignoring her brother. She rested her elbows on the window ledge and stared out at the clouds. Wisps of white floated past, brushing against the window like tattered lace. As they touched the glass, they left a haze of vapor behind, like breath on a mirror. Far below, the ground slid past, a checkered quilt of fenced fields, matchbook-sized buildings, and ribbonlike roads. A train chugged along the straight black line that was its track, leaving a smudge of soot in its wake.

"Would you like to touch a cloud?" Uncle Nigel asked.

"Could I?" Candace asked.

Uncle Nigel reached down and cranked a lever. Slowly the window slid upward. Candace stuck a hand out, letting it trail through the vapor. The cloud felt cool and damp. She tipped her head out the window and closed her eyes, feeling the cloud brush past her face. This must be what it felt like to ride a pegasus. Aside from the droning engines, of course. She leaned out further, letting the wind pluck at her hair.

Uncle Nigel caught her shoulders and eased her back

inside. "Perhaps we should close the window," he said. "It's a little chilly."

Kenneth grinned at Uncle Nigel from the pilot's seat. "When we get to the Moorlands, I'm going to catch a troll," he declared. "And win that contest."

Candace sniffed. "No you're not. I am. When the judges at the *Times* see my pixie—"

"Children!" Uncle Nigel interrupted, halting the argument before it got any further. "Neither one of you will be catching anything, unless it's a cold. Sneaking a ride in a dirigible is one thing, but chasing dangerous creatures across the Moorlands is quite another. It's a region of unhealthy mists and treacherous bogs. When we land, you'll remain on board the dirigible. You'll stay there until I've caught my will o' the wisp, and then we'll go straight home again."

"But I thought—" Kenneth protested.

"But you said—" Candace cried.

Uncle Nigel stared down at them. "I *said* you could come for a ride in my dirigible."

"But I've got all the gear for troll hunting," Kenneth said. "I brought a chain and everything."

"I see," Uncle Nigel said. "That would explain the extra ballast that had to be removed when we lifted off. All that extra weight. Not to mention you two—the pair of you must have eaten a hearty breakfast."

Candace gave her brother a smug look. "Pixies don't weigh much at all," she told Uncle Nigel. "Not like great huge *trolls*."

Kenneth's eyes blazed back at her.

"You two will stay aboard the dirigible, and that's final," said Uncle Nigel.

"Yes, Uncle," Candace murmured, although she had no intention of doing any such thing. As soon as Uncle Nigel went off to catch his will o' the wisp, she'd retrieve her cream and saucer and go pixie hunting.

"And don't be thinking you can sneak off," Uncle Nigel continued. "Old Tom will be keeping an eye on you. And he's got eyes in the back of his head."

Several hours later, the Moorlands came into view below. They were a wide expanse of predominantly flat ground, dotted with low bushes and the occasional large rock. Most of the ground was a mossy green, except for where the peat had been cut away. These patches were rectangular and dark brown, almost black, some of them edged with what looked like low walls: the stacked squares of cut peat.

Up ahead, a large expanse of standing water reflected the red light of the setting sun. It seemed to Kenneth a lonely, empty sort of place. Off in the distance, he could see a solitary peat cutter's stone cottage, but there were no roads leading to it, no towns, no large buildings.

Uncle Nigel spun the wheel and the dirigible nosed down toward the ground. Ahead was a makeshift mooring mast, a rough-cut vertical pole, the bottom of which was attached to a wooden crosspiece weighted down by a pile of stones. About a dozen men waited near it, lounging around a pony-drawn cart that held shovels and other peat-cutting tools. As the dirigible approached them, a small man with thick gray hair and muttonchop sideburns shouted directions. The other men sprang to life, running to grab the lines that trailed from the dirigible's nose. Tugging on these, they guided the dirigible toward the mooring mast as Uncle Nigel halted the engines.

The gray-haired man grabbed the rope attached to the nose of the dirigible and, holding it in his teeth, scrambled up the mast—which, Kenneth could see now, had rungs like a ladder. He fastened the rope to the top of it, then gave a whistle. The other men hauled on the remaining ropes, hand over hand, drawing the dirigible down. Kenneth peered down through the window at them, admiring the way they worked. One day, he'd be just as strong.

As the gondola settled on the ground with a gentle thump, Uncle Nigel threw open the door. He waited while the men lifted large stones into the gondola, under the direction of the gray-haired man. When there was enough ballast on board, Uncle Nigel strode down the stairs toward where the group's leader stood, cap in hand. He was a strange-looking character, with shaggy gray hair down past his collar, those thick sideburns, and eyebrows that jutted out in tufts as stiff as paintbrush bristles. His eyes were a deep brown, almost black. Like the peat cutters, he wore simple brown trousers and a white collarless shirt with rolled-up sleeves that exposed his hairy arms. As Uncle Nigel approached, the man gave him a formal bow.

"Tom!" Uncle Nigel cried. "Jolly good to see you again. How have you been?"

"Very well, Herr Owen."

Uncle Nigel turned back to Candace and Kenneth. "Old Tom and I met in Germany a dozen years back, during my expedition to capture changelings. He helped me sniff out their burrows. He's a good fellow, as solid a man as any I know." He glanced at the make-shift mooring mast. "I knew he'd come up with some-thing to make the landing possible."

Old Tom smiled. "*Danke*, Herr Owen."

"Tom, I'd like you to meet my nephew, Kenneth."

Old Tom inclined his head. "Herr Kenneth."

"And my niece, Candace."

"*Fraulein.*" Old Tom turned to Uncle Nigel. "Will they be assisting you this evening?"

Uncle Nigel laughed. "Definitely not," he said firmly. "They'll be staying right here, in the gondola." He clapped a hand on Old Tom's shoulder. "And you, my dear Tom, will be making sure they remain there."

"I, Herr Owen?"

Uncle Nigel nodded. "Of course, Tom. Who else?"

Old Tom glanced at the men who were securing the dirigible. "Perhaps one of the peat cutters—?"

Uncle Nigel shook his head. "These children are very dear to me, Tom. I need someone I can trust. Implicitly."

Old Tom shifted uncomfortably. "But Herr Owen, I cannot. I have . . . business I must attend to." He glanced toward the eastern horizon, as if he'd seen something there that made him nervous. Kenneth glanced out the window in that direction, but didn't see anything.

"Business?" Uncle Nigel exclaimed, his hand falling away from Old Tom's shoulder. "Out here, on the moors?" He chuckled. "Surely it can wait one night. The Moorlands are a dangerous place; I don't want these two sneaking off." He paused. "I know I can count on you, Tom."

Old Tom stared at his feet. "*Ja*, Herr Owen. But children? I have no knowledge of children."

"It will only be for tonight," Uncle Nigel said in a confident voice. "Catching a will o' the wisp shouldn't take long. They only come out at night, after all. I expect to be back at the dirigible shortly after dawn, whether I've succeeded in bagging one or not. The children will no doubt spend most of the time sleeping." He fixed Kenneth and Candace with a steely eye. "Won't you, children?"

Kenneth, who had been about to clamber out of the gondola, paused with one foot on the top step. He felt Candace's hand clench his jacket and tug him back.

"Oh, yes," Candace said quickly.

Kenneth nearly rolled his eyes. He raised his arms above his head, as if stretching. He added a fake yawn for good measure.

Behind him, Candace hissed in his ear. "You're overdoing it."

Kenneth elbowed her. She let go of his jacket.

Uncle Nigel clapped his hands together. "Now then," he said, his voice brisk. "Let's place some more ballast on board and get my gear loaded onto the cart. See to it, Tom. And make sure the men don't dent the antenna or slop acid out of the batteries. If they're ruined, I'll have to use the ones from the dirigible—and I won't be happy about that."

"*Ja*, Herr Owen," he answered, glancing once again at the east. Then he scowled at Candace and Kenneth. It was clear he didn't like children. And that he took his responsibilities to Uncle Nigel seriously.

Sneaking away with him watching them was going to be tough.

Hours later, Kenneth stared across the moonlit gondola at Old Tom, wondering if what Uncle Nigel had said might be true about Old Tom having eyes in the back of his head. Old Tom's hair was thick and bushy, and for all Kenneth knew, there just might be eyes back there. He certainly looked around smartly enough whenever Kenneth or Candace stirred on the mattress they shared on the floor.

He reminded Kenneth of a dog watching two cats. He even chewed on the ivory stem of his unlit pipe like a dog worrying a bone.

Old Tom didn't seem inclined toward sleep. He'd watched as the peat cutters began the long walk back to their cottages, tools over their shoulders, and as Uncle Nigel departed in the cart they'd filled with his creature-catching gear. Now Old Tom sat in the pilot's chair, staring out the window toward the east, watching the moon rise.

Kenneth concentrated on making his breathing slow and deep, just like Candace, who seemed to have genuinely fallen asleep. Meanwhile, he kept his eyes open the tiniest slit, watching Old Tom's back. And waiting.

Eventually, Old Tom eased his boots off his feet. Kenneth's heart beat a little faster; surely Old Tom was getting ready to go to sleep. Then the gondola shifted slightly as Old Tom rose from his seat and crossed to where the twins lay. He paused, his feet just in front of Kenneth's face. Kenneth was surprised to see that Old Tom wasn't wearing stockings, then realized that the man's toenails—long and white—would have cut holes in the toes of any stockings he put on.

Kenneth scrunched his eyes shut as Old Tom leaned over him. The old man prodded Kenneth's shoulder with the stem of his pipe. Then he straightened and walked away.

A moment later, Kenneth heard the gondola's door open, then close. The dirigible lifted slightly, as if someone had stepped off.

Almost immediately, Candace sat up.

Kenneth opened his eyes in alarm. "What are you doing?" he hissed at his sister. He looked around the cabin, but Old Tom was nowhere in sight. He really had exited the gondola.

Candace shook her head. "He's gone out to have a smoke," she said. She rolled her eyes. "About time, too. I had to keep pinching myself to stay awake."

"It could be a trick," Kenneth said. "Old Tom could be waiting just outside, to see what we do. Stay where you are." Tossing off his blanket, he crept on hands and knees toward the door.

To his irritation, Candace followed. Together, they eased the door open and peered outside. Old Tom was running away across the moor, his jacket half pulled up over his head. He gave a strange little hop, then stumbled and fell. Hurling aside his jacket, he staggered to his feet and kept running.

"How curious," Candace breathed.

Kenneth nodded—then realized he was agreeing with his sister. "He must have a good reason for acting so strangely," he whispered.

Suddenly, it occurred to him what that reason might be. He glanced nervously up through the open door at the hydrogen-filled bag, afraid that a spark from Old Tom's pipe might have settled there. A fire would explain why the fellow was running away in such a panic. But there was no smell of tobacco in the air. The pipe lay on the ground just beyond the gondola steps, unlit.

Candace, meanwhile, seemed unconcerned with the potential dangers. She hurried to the cabinet that she'd tossed her bag into earlier. Suddenly realizing that Old

Tom might turn around and run back to the dirigible at any moment, Kenneth raced to haul his sack out of its hiding place. He and Candace both made it back to the door at the same time, and elbowed each other in their hurry to be the first out. They tumbled down the steps together, landing on the ground in a heap. The dirigible rose slightly, and the line that held it to the mast creaked.

Kenneth picked himself up and slung his sack over one shoulder. He glanced out across the Moorlands. It was a wide expanse of empty ground, without a cottage in sight. Scruffy-looking bushes cast odd shadows in the moonlight. Mosquitoes filled the air with a high-pitched whine, and a low mist swirled around Kenneth's ankles. The air felt damp and smelled faintly of rot.

Kenneth shivered. This was no place for a girl to be wandering about on her own. He decided to ask Candace if she'd like to come along with him. Candace could keep the prize if he won the contest; Kenneth didn't want the silly book, anyway. He just wanted to see the looks on the other boys' faces when he told them he'd bagged a troll.

He turned to Candace. "If you'd like, I could—"

"Tag along with me?" she asked, guessing—incorrectly—at what he'd been about to say. She sniffed disdainfully. "Don't even *think* of it. That stupid, clanking sack will just scare away the pixies. If you're scared, then stay here at the dirigible. *I'm* going creature catching."

Kenneth bristled. "Look who's calling who scared," he snapped. He could see the nervous way Candace was looking around. She was twisting a strand of her hair—something she did when she was feeling anxious. She didn't want to venture out alone on the Moorlands, either.

"Me?" Candace said in an exaggerated voice, touching a hand to her chest like an actress. "Scared?" She sniffed again. "*I'm* big enough to take care of myself. I don't need help from any boy. Especially my brother."

Kenneth ground his teeth. Candace was starting to sound just like Mother. And once again, she'd found a way to comment on how short he was. But you didn't need to be big to make your way in the world. Gentleman Jim had proven that when he used the science of pugilism to triumph over the larger John Sullivan, laying him low with a knockout punch in the twenty-first round.

Kenneth squared his shoulders and marched briskly away from the dirigible, leaving Candace behind before she could utter another insulting word. Just as Gentleman Jim had done, Kenneth was about to take on a heavyweight.

Heavy as stone.

Candace walked across the Moorlands, her bag in hand. Inside the bag, the bottle of cream clinked gently against the saucer. Although she could see the dirigible in the distance, the moors were a lonely place. The moonlight turned everything to shades of black and gray, and a pale white mist shifted around her ankles as she walked. The ground was soft, and pockmarked by the shallow trenches left behind by the peat cutters. Some of these looked like half-dug graves, the slabs of peat stacked beside them forming their headstones.

From the distance came a mournful howl.

"Wolves," Candace whispered, her eyes wide. She clutched the bag to her chest, wishing Kenneth were with her. She couldn't see any sign of her brother, however. Which shouldn't have been surprising. She'd deliberately walked in the opposite direction to the one he'd taken; the dirigible was between them now. There was also no sign of Old Tom, or Uncle Nigel. Candace was very much alone.

For several long moments, she stood, listening. Had the wolf howled a second time, she probably would have dropped her bag and run back to the dirigible. But as the silence stretched longer and longer, her nerve returned. To turn around now was to resign herself to a life of obscurity. In order to be *somebody*, she needed to capture a pixie and win the *Londinium Times* contest. Years from now, when the biographers wrote the story of Lady Candace Owen's life, they would point to this very night as a turning point. Her pixie would be the first exquisite specimen in the gardens that would bear her name and be her lasting legacy.

"That wasn't a wolf howling," she told herself

firmly. "It was a hound. One of the peat cutters is out hunting with a hound."

She didn't quite believe it, of course. But it made her feel a little better.

She trudged on, looking for pixies. She'd expected to see signs of them by now. Uncle Nigel had said they were as numerous as the mosquitoes that Candace kept having to shoo away from her face, but there didn't seem to be any out dancing under the moon tonight. Instead of mushroom rings, all Candace could see when she looked at the ground were the glittering trails left by slugs. All in all, the Moorlands had proved one big disappointment.

No . . . just a moment.

Candace crouched down and examined the ground more closely. That wasn't a slug trail, but a line of tiny footprints. Each was the size of a thumbprint and was filled with a dust that shone silver in the moonlight.

Pixie dust.

Excited now, Candace followed the footprints. They led her on a meandering path across the moor, up over stones, and down through the trenches left by the peat cutters. At one point they disappeared under a clump of heather, but by circling around it, Candace picked up the trail again on the other side.

She kept expecting the footprints to lead her to a tiny stone cottage, or a hole in the ground, or wherever it was that pixies made their home, but instead they kept going. After a while, the footprints became irregularly spaced, as if the pixie had been hopping or skipping, instead of walking along. The trail curved around in a wide circle, only to meet up with the original path once more. There, the footprints abruptly ended.

Candace set her bag on the ground and crouched down, looking for any sign of where the pixie might have gone. Had it gone back the way it had come, in an attempt to fool her? She didn't think so. The ground was soft here; she could see the imprint left by each individual toe of the tiny, bare feet. The pixie would have needed to walk precisely in its own footprints—backwards—to retrace its steps and go back the way it had come. It must instead have used magic to disappear. But why, if it could vanish like this at any point, had it bothered to skip around in a circle first?

As she pondered this riddle, Candace noticed that the earth between the footprints looked rough, almost as though it had been laid with tiny cobblestones. Peering closely at them, she saw that the "cobblestones" were in fact the tops of mushrooms. Each was tiny—the size of a baby's button—but even as Candace watched, they grew. Within a few minutes, the mushroom stalks were as tall as wooden matches.

"A faerie ring," Candace whispered. "Seeded with pixie dust, and watered by moonlight."

The pixie hadn't been skipping when it had made the circle; it had been dancing. And a ring of mushrooms had grown where its feet had trod.

But why had it chosen this spot to dance?

Candace stood up and glanced around. The circle

the pixie had created was easily the size of a riding arena. Near its center was a pile of stones. Stepping carefully over the mushroom ring, she walked toward the stones. As she drew closer, she saw that they had once been part of a peat cutter's cottage. The thatch roof had long since blown away and the walls were no more than a waist-high jumble of stones, but the slab that formed the front step was in place. Perhaps, years ago, the peat cutter had set out cream there for the pixie. And the pixie had remembered that and returned to dance around the ruined hut of its former friend.

Candace took the saucer out of her bag and set it on the step. She uncorked the cream and poured until the saucer was full. Then she set the bottle down and looked around for a place to sit and wait. She didn't want the pixie to see her right away. It needed to drink the cream first; that's how it would know she wanted to be its friend.

She walked around the side of the ruined cottage and settled herself with her back against the stones. As she waited for the pixie to return, she yawned. She needed to stay awake. She glanced up at the stars, trying to remember the names of the constellations. There was Orion the Hunter, and there, the Plough. She yawned again and rubbed her eyes; she was too tired to remember more names. She hoped she wouldn't have to wait long for the pixie; she needed to get back to the dirigible by dawn, so Uncle Nigel wouldn't worry about her being gone. She'd walked a long way, but she

thought she could manage to get back in time, as long as the pixie came soon.

It didn't. The mist shifted across the moors, the stars and moon crept across the sky, and the mosquitoes continued to hum. Eventually, Candace decided to lie down and rest her head on her bag. Just for a little while.

Her eyes closed.

A mosquito bit her. She slapped it. Sleepily, she opened her eyes and stared across the moonlit moors. Still no pixies.

Her eyes closed again.

On the other side of the ruined cottage, a tiny creature crept out of a space between two of the fallen stones and began lapping at the cream.

Candace slept.

4

Kenneth woke with a start, his pocketknife clutched in his hand. He sat up and listened intently, but heard only the steady buzzing of mosquitoes. The howling that had frightened him earlier in the night had stopped.

He sat up and folded his knife shut, then rubbed his eyes. Waving away the mosquitoes, he looked around. The moon was slipping below the western horizon, and in the east the sky was turning pink. Good. He'd managed to wake up exactly when he'd hoped to, just before dawn. The trolls would be rambling around the moors, but in a few minutes' time, when the sun cleared the horizon, they'd all turn to stone.

His chain and padlock lay on the ground beside him; he'd dumped them out and used the sack as a makeshift blanket to keep out the ground's chill. Now he shook off the sack and stuffed the chain and lock back into it. Then he stood. The dirigible was a distant white lump on the landscape, too far away to be able to tell if anyone was stirring around it. Kenneth wondered if Candace had given up on pixie hunting and gone back to wait for Uncle Nigel. She'd probably tell their uncle that Kenneth alone had disobeyed his order not to leave the dirigible—pretending all the while to have been a good girl by staying put. Kenneth shook his head. Surely Uncle Nigel would appreciate the fact that he was a boy who didn't meekly sit about when there was adventure to be had.

He decided he'd worry about that later. The question of the moment was how to find a troll.

Last night he'd assumed it would be a simple matter of choosing a suitable spot with an unobstructed view over the moors, then waiting for a troll to amble by and following it. Trolls were large, stupid creatures that probably wouldn't notice someone following them. Yes, they were dangerous—nearly twice the height of a grown man, with broad shoulders and chests that would put a heavyweight boxer to shame. But according to the boys at school, they lumbered about with ponderous, heavy steps. If a troll did spot Kenneth, it would be an easy matter to run away from it.

Yet Kenneth hadn't seen any trolls last night. The few promising shapes he had spotted had all turned out, upon closer inspection, to be nothing more than large boulders. Just like the one that stood over there on the left, for example. In the twilight it looked, for all the world, like a large figure hunkered down in a squat, arms wrapped around its knees and chin on its chest.

Just a moment . . .

That boulder hadn't been there last night, when Kenneth had lain down to sleep.

It must be a troll!

Excitement pounding through him, Kenneth dropped into a crouch behind a clump of heather. Peering over it, he studied the boulder. As the sky lightened, he could make out the contours of the arms and legs, the lump of a nose, and the bulges that were the creature's closed eyes. The troll's skin was a mottled gray, the color of granite.

It seemed to be asleep.

Kenneth waited in nervous silence as the sun slowly rose above the moors. Eventually a ray of sunlight touched the creature, throwing a long black shadow behind it. Kenneth expected to see some sort of change occur, but the troll looked the same as before, even though the sunlight had certainly, by now, turned it to solid stone.

Clutching his sack, Kenneth circled around behind the troll. The spot where it squatted was boggy; the heavy creature had sunk to its ankles in the soft ground. A wide, shallow puddle had seeped out of the peat and surrounded the troll on all sides. The troll was enormous. Standing up, it would probably be twice the height of a man. Kenneth moved slowly, wary of making any splashing noises, in case the troll hadn't quite finished turning to stone yet. When he got close enough, he leaned forward and touched its broad back gingerly with a finger. The skin felt rough and cool, like stone, but it wasn't entirely hard. Kenneth's finger dented it slightly.

The troll didn't move.

It didn't have any ears, just a hole in either side of its head. Nor did it have hair. A large bump on its right shoulder turned out to be a sparrow's nest. Four tiny fledglings with bright yellow beaks peeped out of the nest and stared down at Kenneth, then ducked out of sight again.

The nest was a good sign; the troll must be slow moving indeed for it not to have fallen off.

Feeling a little braver now, Kenneth knocked on the troll's broad back. It was solid and hard. Definitely stone.

Squelching around to the front of the troll, Kenneth pulled the chain and padlock from his sack. The way the troll was squatting, arms wrapped around its legs, meant that its hands were close together. Kenneth looped the chain around its wrists—each nearly as thick as Kenneth's waist—and then around the troll's ankles. Then he readied the padlock. Holding the key in his mouth, he clambered onto one of the troll's lumpy knees and reached for the two ends of chain. All he had to do now was padlock them together. Then he could run back to the dirigible and announce to Uncle Nigel that he'd bagged a troll.

He grinned. The contest was as good as won.

Kenneth was just slipping the padlock through the two end links of chain when something swooped past his head, startling him. The key fell from his mouth, landing with a splash in the water between the troll's feet. A second later, he heard the fledglings cheeping loudly and realized he'd been startled by the mother sparrow returning to her nest.

Clambering down from the troll's knee, Kenneth felt about in the puddle. The water was murky; he couldn't see the key. The more he groped for it, the more mud he stirred up.

The fledgling sparrows continued cheeping, demanding that their mother feed them. But the mother sparrow had been bothered by seeing Kenneth; she flew round and round the troll, refusing to land. Kenneth, meanwhile, kept feeling about in the soft muddy bottom of the puddle for the key, but all he could feel were the troll's big lumpy toes.

Then the troll's left foot shifted.

Kenneth glanced up in alarm—just in time to see the troll's eyes open.

Quick as any human, the troll yanked its hands out of the loops of chain. One hand went up to wave the sparrow away. The other grabbed Kenneth.

Kenneth yelped in surprise as stony fingers fastened on his shoulder, bunching up his jacket and lifting him from the ground. The troll stood, teetered, nearly fell—then yanked one foot free of the chain. Waving the mother sparrow off with its free hand, it shifted its weight and flicked the chain away with an angry kick of its other foot. Then it lifted Kenneth closer to its huge, round eyes. They looked like enormous glass marbles—clear, with a swirl of gray in the middle.

"You're . . . you're supposed to be turned to stone!" Kenneth cried. He twisted in the troll's grip. The troll's fingers tightened, bruising his shoulder. Kenneth managed to wriggle half out of his jacket and almost got free, but then the troll tossed him up in the air and caught him in a firmer grip around the middle, squeezing the air from his lungs.

Kenneth glanced at the sun—fully above the horizon now—and back at the troll. It grinned at him with a mouth full of quartz-crystal teeth that sparkled in the morning light. Kenneth knew he'd made a horrible, horrible mistake. The boys at school had been wrong. Trolls *didn't* turn to stone in sunlight.

And now it looked as though this one was going to eat him—assuming Kenneth didn't die of asphyxiation first.

"Please," Kenneth managed to wheeze. "I can't . . . breathe."

The troll tossed Kenneth in the air a second time, flipping him. This time, it caught him by one ankle. Blood rushed to Kenneth's head as he dangled upside down. The troll's hand was clamped around his left ankle like a manacle. Kenneth flailed at the troll but didn't manage to hit it.

The fledglings continued their manic cheeping. Their mother circled frantically around the troll's head.

The troll's eyes narrowed. It glanced at the bird and grumbled, grinding its quartz teeth. Then it shifted its attention back to Kenneth, lifting him up to eye level. The ground seemed terribly far below Kenneth's head.

The troll's mouth opened. Its breath smelled of peat.

"Please!" Kenneth begged. "Don't eat me!" His entire body was trembling now. This was it. He was going to die. Just one month after his eleventh birthday, and he was going to die. He swallowed down a lump in his throat and blinked furiously, trying not to cry. "Just put me down—there's a good fellow—and I'll leave you alone," he pleaded. "I'll go away and never bother you again."

"Bother," the troll repeated in a low, gravelly voice.

Kenneth gasped. He'd thought trolls were too stupid to speak. Then again, the troll might have just been mimicking the word, as a parrot will. On the other hand, maybe it really *did* have a dim understanding what Kenneth was trying to tell it.

"Down," Kenneth continued, keeping it simple. Blood pounded in his ears; hanging upside down was making him dizzy. He pointed past his head at the ground, and spoke as slowly and firmly as he could. "Put . . . me . . . on . . . ground."

"Ground?" the troll rumbled, glancing down.

"Yes," Kenneth exclaimed. The troll did understand! "Me—" he tapped his chest, "go ground." He gestured down. "You—" he pointed at the troll, "let go . . ." He made a show of opening his hand, as if releasing something. "Hand. Me . . ." He waved in the general direction of the dirigible. "Leave."

The troll frowned. It absently scratched its chin with a finger, causing a sound like two bricks rubbing together. "Why thee speak sae strange?"

"I—" Kenneth halted, surprised. The troll's voice was slow and rumbling, but there had been no hesitations between its words.

The troll peered more closely at Kenneth. "Are thee gormless?" it asked.

"What?"

"Gormless," the troll repeated slowly. "Daft." It tapped a finger against its forehead. "Nae sae bright."

Kenneth understood. The troll was calling him stupid. "Hardly!" he sputtered. His penmanship might be shaky, but he was top of his class in geography; he could name the capital city of any country you pleased. Neither of which mattered right now, of course. The most pressing issue for Kenneth, at the moment, was to not be eaten. And to get the troll to set him down before he fainted from all the blood rushing to his head.

"I just didn't realize you spoke English," Kenneth said.

"Oh, aye?" the troll said.

"And speak it quite well, I might add," Kenneth continued. "Now . . . how about setting me down?"

"Tha' chain," the troll rumbled. "Was it thee put it roun' me ankles?"

"Ah . . . n—"

The troll glowered.

"Yes," Kenneth admitted. "Yes, it was."

"Why thee dunnit?"

"Why do you think?" Kenneth asked, exasperated. "I'm a creature catcher. That's what we do—catch creatures."

The troll considered this. "Oh, aye?" it said again. "Why'd thee choose me?"

Kenneth shrugged. "Because . . . well, because you were the only troll I could find."

The troll chuckled. From its stomach came a low, grumbling noise. A hungry sound.

Kenneth suddenly regretted his bravado. "Are—" he swallowed. "Are you going to eat me?"

"P'rhaps," the troll said with a sly grin. "Let's see 'ow thee taste." He tiled his head back and opened his mouth wide, then lifted Kenneth above it. A tongue, rough as a grindstone, brushed Kenneth's ear and cheek.

"Ouch!" Kenneth cried, shrinking back from the tongue. He twisted around and flailed a hand in the general direction of the dirigible. "That's my uncle's dirigible. My uncle is Nigel Owen, the famous creature catcher. If you hurt me, Uncle Nigel will hunt you down and chain you up and . . . and . . ."

The troll laughed.

Kenneth's head spun. He felt well and truly queasy now; he'd been upside down too long. "Oh no," he groaned. "I think I'm going to be sick."

An instant later, he was lying on the ground. The troll had set him down. Kenneth forced himself to his feet and raised his fists. He wasn't going to let a little queasiness knock him out of the fight. "I warn you," he told the troll. "I know how to box. Let me go or you'll regret it."

"Fancy a bray, do ye?" the troll rumbled. It spread its

arms wide. "Get on wi' it, then. Gi' me a skelpin'." It winked. "If thee can upskittle me, I'll let thee go."

Kenneth bounced lightly on the balls of his feet, his fists raised, limbering up. He took a deep breath, blew it out, dodged to one side of the troll, then danced back to its front again, keeping his footwork light and his fists up to guard his face. The troll simply stared at him, unmoving. Kenneth kept up his footwork, trying to decide where to punch. The troll's entire body was hard as stone. Throwing a punch at it would leave Kenneth with skinned knuckles, possibly even a broken hand.

The troll chuckled—a sound like gravel rattling in a stone cup. "Well?" it demanded.

Kenneth glanced back at the dirigible, hoping that Uncle Nigel might have returned to it and come looking for him, but there was no one there. No sign of Old Tom, either.

"I'm near famished," the troll said, its jagged teeth glinting wickedly. "So if thee's done muckin' about—"

The mother sparrow circled around the troll's head, then landed on the nest, setting off a flurry of cheeping. The troll turned its head to grimace at the fledglings.

Kenneth turned and bolted.

His feet slipped in the puddle, but fear propelled him out of it. He sprinted as he had never done before, toward the distant dirigible. Behind him, he heard the troll curse, then a great sucking noise as its feet left the boggy puddle. The damp ground quivered as the troll ran after him, its heavy feet slamming down onto the earth. Kenneth ran even faster, arms and legs pumping, not daring to look behind him as the thudding foot-steps got closer, and quicker, and still closer . . .

An enormous hand slammed into Kenneth's back, knocking him headlong to the ground. When he stopped tumbling, he lifted his head and shook it groggily, spitting out peat.

The troll stomped up beside him. It prodded Kenneth gently—probably not wanting to damage its meal—then clamped a hand around Kenneth's arm and yanked him to his feet.

"Don't," it rumbled, "try tha' again."

Candace felt something brush against her hand. She stirred, not quite awake. She was having such a lovely dream. In it, she was cutting the ribbon to officially open Lady Candace Owen's Public Gardens. Lady Hawthorne stood at the front of the assembled dignitaries, applauding politely. The Queen stood next to her, wearing her usual black dress and bonnet. Then the dream changed.

Someone tugged on Candace's left hand, preventing her from cutting the ribbon. Candace glanced to the side, and saw that it was her mother who gripped her hand. Mother was carrying a padlock and chain; she wanted Candace to come and chain herself to the railing outside the Parliament Buildings—a favorite protest tactic of the suffrage movement. Except that it wasn't Mother but Kenneth who had Candace's hand, since Candace had become a troll. And Kenneth didn't care if she ever got the vote. He just wanted to lock her up in a zoo . . .

Candace rolled over, trying to steer her dream in a more pleasant direction. Her bag didn't make a very good pillow; it was too lumpy. And her mosquito bites were itching. Eyes closed, she nudged the cloth bag flatter, then nested her cheek back into it again.

Something tugged on her hand. Something with hands just barely big enough to wrap around her thumb.

Candace's eyes sprang open.

A tiny man, no more than ankle-high, was tugging on her thumb. He wore a gray, furry vest and trousers that looked as though they were made out of mouse skin, and a cap made from the top of an acorn. His feet were bare. His face was as puckered as a dried apple, and his skin was a pale green.

"A pixie!" Candace breathed. She sat up slowly, so as not to frighten him.

The pixie showed no signs of fear. He let go of her thumb, tilted his head, and smiled. His teeth were as yellow as buttercup petals. So were his eyes.

Candace stole a glance at the saucer she'd set out. It was empty.

"Did you enjoy the cream?" she asked. "Master—?" She paused, waiting for the pixie to supply his name. If he did, it would be a mark of true friendship; the *Girl's Own Annual* had said pixies only told their names to those they trusted.

The pixie began picking his nose.

Candace glanced away, not certain where to look. The *Girl's Own* hadn't mentioned anything like this. It had said pixies were beautiful—and, one would presume from that, polite. This pixie wasn't the prettiest creature Candace had seen—it certainly didn't look anything like the illustration in the *Girl's Own*—but then maybe he was old and hard of hearing. That would explain why he hadn't given his name. He *was* a pixie, though; his feet had left silvery footprints where he'd walked. He just wasn't what Candace expected.

The pixie flicked a glob of mucus from his finger. The finger returned to his nose again and resumed its digging. "Oo'r you?" he said around it.

She curtsied. "Candace Owen. And you are—?"

The pixie once again ignored her invitation to supply his name. He withdrew his finger and wiped it on his vest, then extended his weathered hand to Candace. "Fancy a dance?" he asked.

Candace hesitated. Those fingers didn't look very clean. Dancing with the little fellow, however, would be a way of earning his trust. It was morning already; the sun was peeping above the horizon. Uncle Nigel would be returning to the dirigible soon and would realize she had disobeyed his order to stay put. Candace was going to get in trouble, no matter what, so she might as well not return to the dirigible empty-handed.

She bent down and extended her index finger. The pixie grasped it firmly in both hands. He backed away with an odd little skip, and Candace took a step to follow him. Grinning, he skipped a few more steps; Candace followed. Bent over as she was, it was hard to manage anything but a shuffling step, but the pixie didn't seem to mind. He started to whistle—a strange little off-key melody that sounded somehow playful and sad at the same time.

From all around Candace came answering whistles. Looking about, she saw that the mushrooms had grown since she'd slept; they were as tall as her ankle now, their white stalks as thick as broom handles and their red caps nearly as wide as saucers. The whistling sound came from behind these.

"Are there other pixies here?" Candace asked.

The pixie winked at her and continued dancing backwards, pulling her along.

Candace trotted after him as he led her in a circle around the ruined cottage. He moved at a fair clip; it was hard to keep from tripping. Her feet seemed to want to go in time with the melody he was whistling, which was fast and complicated. It was a dance meant for tiny, nimble feet, not those of a human. She was glad she wasn't wearing her corset; with it laced tight around her waist, she'd never have been able to catch her breath. Or even bend over.

"I was wondering," Candace puffed as they circled around the far side of the ruined cottage, "if you'd like to go on a grand adventure." She pointed with her free hand at the dirigible, the gas bag of which had turned a lovely pink in the morning sun. "That's my Uncle Nigel's dirigible. He'll be returning to Londinium in it later today, once he's caught a will o' the wisp. I'll be going with him. Would you like to come along?"

The pixie continued whistling. They were passing the front of the ruined cottage now, and the spot where the empty saucer sat on the doorstep. Candace couldn't see any footprints on the step, nor was the pixie making any now; the pixie dust must have only been visible in moonlight.

Out of the corner of her eye, she saw movement behind several of the mushroom stalks. Wizened green faces peeked out at her as she danced. Watching. Waiting.

When Candace reached the spot where she'd been sleeping, the pixie abruptly let go of her hand and stopped whistling. The others stopped whistling as well. Candace stood, hands on her hips, breathing quickly.

"You don't need to hide," she told the other pixies. "I'm not going to hurt you."

She heard laughter. Then, one by one, the pixies stepped into view.

There seemed to be about a dozen of them. They were all about the same size as the one that had just danced with Candace, with the same bright yellow eyes and teeth. Some were male, some female, but all had weathered, wrinkled faces and pale hair the color of straw. Candace wondered if they were all old, or if pixies were born looking that way. Some wore mouse-fur trousers and capes made from woven grass. Others had draped themselves in faded scraps of cloth—probably rags scavenged from the peat cutters' trash heaps.

As the pixies drew nearer, Candace crouched down to make herself appear smaller. She didn't want to intimidate the tiny folk. They seemed to have no fear of her, however. Tiny hands plucked at the laces of her boots or fingered the hem of her dress, feeling its texture.

"You're just the size of my dolls," Candace observed. She gave them a smile, but was careful not to bare her teeth. That had always been Kenneth's mistake with Mrs. Soames's dog: using his teeth to smile at it. Dogs saw that as a challenge.

"If one of you should care to come home with me," she continued, "he or she will have lots of lovely clothes. And a quaint little dollhouse to live in, with dear little chairs and tables that are just your size. I could put it out back on the lawn, next to a tall, shady oak tree. You'd feel right at home there."

She waited beside the ruined cottage, trying not to appear too hopeful. It was hard to appear calm when one's heart was pounding with excitement. In another moment, she'd have done it. Captured a pixie—not with a nasty trap, but simply by becoming its friend.

The pixies glanced at one another, exchanging quick words in a language Candace didn't understand. Their voices sounded like the squeaking of mice. One of the female pixies fingered Candace's stocking, then bent closer and sniffed at her ankle. That pixie nodded, grinning, at her companions.

"Well?" Candace asked. She was starting to worry that Kenneth might have been right about them not speaking English. Maybe she *should* have brought along a Welsh-English dictionary. But actions could speak as eloquently as words, and there was something she *had* brought along that just might do the trick. She turned and tried to take a step to the spot where her bag lay—and found herself skipping there, instead. Strange, that. But she didn't have time to worry about it just now.

Reaching into the bag, she pulled out a white, lace-trimmed handkerchief that was tied in a knot. Untying it, she let it fall open against the palm of her hand. Inside were a dozen buttons, some made from pearl and others of fancy brass. Candace had found them in Daisy's sewing kit; she hoped the maid wouldn't be angry. Candace crouched again, offering them to the pixies.

One of the male pixies touched a corner of the hankie with a grubby hand. The others crowded closer, forming a circle around Candace.

"That's right," Candace said encouragingly. "The buttons are for you. A present. Aren't they pretty?" She started to turn, in order to show the others the buttons, but the pixie who had touched the hankie suddenly grabbed it and yanked it out of her hand, sending the buttons tumbling to the ground.

"Oh, don't!" Candace exclaimed.

The pixie leaped away from her, holding the hand-kerchief.

"I'm sorry," Candace said immediately. "Did my cry startle you? There, there, don't worry, I—"

The pixie squeaked something at her. Then he waved the hankie above his head like a captured flag while the others answered him in their strange language. One of them grabbed a corner of the waving hankie, and then a second and a third. A four-way tug-of-war ensued. Soon all of the pixies were tugging on it, squeaking furiously at each other all the while. One of them leaped onto the middle of the handkerchief, and then another, and then the hankie disappeared under a host of diving bodies, all elbowing and kicking each other. Candace heard a tearing noise; a moment later one of the pixies emerged with a muddy tatter of white lace clenched between her teeth. The buttons, ignored, were trampled into the earth.

"You needn't fight!" Candace cried, rising to her feet in alarm. "There's plenty more where that came from. You can *all* come back to Londinium with me, if you like. I've more than one handkerchief, you know."

The pixies ignored her, continuing to tumble and fight. Or rather, most of them did. Candace felt a sharp poke in the back of her right leg and turned to see the pixie that had danced with her. He stood, a stick in one hand, staring up at her. Then he poked her again. Harder.

"Hey!" Candace exclaimed, jumping back.

The pixie backed up a step.

Candace took a deep breath. It wouldn't do to get cross, she reminded herself. The fellow obviously hadn't meant to hurt her; he just wanted her attention.

"Dance," the pixie said, his frown adding yet another crease to his forehead.

Folding her hands neatly together, Candace spoke in a calm, soothing voice. "I'd love to dance with you, Master Pixie. But how about taking a little walk with me first, over to the dirigible? Perhaps we could dance once we reach it, and I could introduce you to my uncle." She crouched and extended her hand, inviting him to take hold of her finger as he had before. Behind her, the other pixies continued their battle over the hankie.

Her pixie friend kept glancing in their direction, then back at Candace again. If she could just get him away from the others, perhaps he would come with her.

The pixie grinned and took hold of Candace's finger. The other pixies fell silent. Out of the corner of her eye, she could see them standing motionless, expectantly watching her, scraps of her torn hankie in their hands.

Candace leaned closer to her friend. "Wouldn't you rather—"

He tugged on her finger, pulling her forward—and suddenly Candace found herself dancing.

The pixies cheered.

The pixie who had tugged her finger let it go. Candace twirled like an Irishman dancing a jig. She tried to stand still but her feet wouldn't stop. They spun her around in a circle—she had to throw out her arms to keep her balance—then did a strange little one-two-three, one-two-three skip-step in place.

Her feet seemed to have a mind of their own. She could move her arms, bend at the waist, or turn her head however she liked, but from the hips down it felt like someone else was moving her body. The pixies, meanwhile, trotted along behind her. Not dancing—just following. Several had sticks in their hands now. They beat these against the ground, keeping time with her dance.

"Please," Candace said, frightened now. "Stop it. Let me go."

The pixies laughed. One of them ran between her dancing feet. Her legs tangled together and she fell. Several of the pixies poked her with their sticks.

"Dance!" they squealed. "Dance!"

They all spoke English, it seemed. Or at least, knew that one word.

Candace lurched to her feet and tried to run back to the dirigible, but her feet betrayed her. They danced her away from the mushroom ring, back into the circle of grinning pixies. Their yellow eyes gleamed expectantly.

"Please," she tried again as her feet kept dancing. "I wasn't going to force any of you to go anywhere you didn't want to. I wasn't going to *capture* you; I wanted to be your friend." The words, however, sounded false to her ears. She knew that, if the pixie had proved too frightened to come on board the dirigible willingly, she'd have scooped him up and put him there—then soothed him once the dirigible was up and away. Assuming he could be soothed. The pixies must have sensed this about her.

"I won't take you home with me, then," she told the

pixie who had danced with her. "I'll just go and find something else for that silly contest."

The pixies had fallen silent now. They leaned on their sticks, watching her with those bright yellow eyes.

Candace twisted around so she could look at the one she'd first danced with. "Please," she begged. "You've had your fun. My feet hurt and I need to rest. Let me go."

He cocked his head. "No," he answered. "You are mine."

The other pixies laughed. Their would-be catcher had been caught.

By now, the sun had fully risen. Candace, still dancing, was getting hot. Perspiration trickled down her face and her breath came in great, unladylike gulps. She just wanted to be away from here. Surely there was some other creature she could capture—something that would respond to a soothing word and meekly follow her back to the dirigible instead of making her dance with it for hours on end.

Her legs felt rubbery now and her feet had begun to ache, but surely the pixies would tire of the dance soon. Eventually, she knew, they would let her go. The tales she'd heard of people meeting pixies and disappearing, never to be seen again, were just that. Silly tales. Pixies were fey folk, just like faeries. And faeries never hurt anyone.

Her feet pattered across the ground, spinning her around in a circle. Now she was facing the ruined cottage. The sun shone in through cracks in the heap of stone, illuminating something inside. Something round and white.

Her feet carried her closer to the ruin. Now she could see the two black holes in the round white thing, and the teeth that lined the bottom of it.

Candace's eyes widened in horror.

The white thing inside the ruined cottage was a human skull.

5

Kenneth trudged along beside the troll, stumbling under the weight of its hand upon his shoulder. He was reminded of the times he'd been marched to the headmaster's office at school, his instructor tugging him along by the ear. Except that this wasn't going to end in a caning.

Kenneth pressed his lips together firmly to keep them from trembling. Why didn't the troll just eat him and be done with it?

"Where are you taking me?" he asked it.

"Tae me burrow," it answered.

Kenneth imagined a hole in the ground, filled with bones and a large, blackened cook pot. And a blood-stained butcher's block. And a meat ax. He had to get away. He had to. But the troll's hand was as heavy on his shoulder as a block of stone. It lumbered along with heavy steps, its feet leaving deep footprints.

They'd walked quite a way, never once getting any closer to the dirigible, although Kenneth could see it in the distance. He'd tried to angle in that direction, but the troll had nudged him back the way it wanted to go. As he walked, Kenneth kept a sharp eye out, hoping to spot Uncle Nigel's cart. Or perhaps Old Tom, if he was still running about the moors. Right now, Kenneth would even welcome a glimpse of Candace.

What he really needed was a weapon. Something he could hurl at the troll to stun it, maybe even knock it senseless, like David did to Goliath. Even creatures with skin like stone must have a weak point. Those eyes, for example. They looked like glass. If Kenneth could shatter one with a stone, surely that would hurt the troll. Maybe even blind it. Then Kenneth could make another run for it. This time, he'd escape.

Spotting a suitable stone on the ground, Kenneth pretended to trip in one of the shallow trenches left by the peat cutters. He landed with one hand on the stone, just as he'd planned. But before he could turn and hurl it, the troll's hand slammed down on top of his.

Its face loomed just above Kenneth's, teeth bared. "What hae thee got there?"

"N-nothing," Kenneth said.

"Oh, aye? Why is tha' cob in thy hand, then?"

"The stone? I'm just—" Kenneth cast wildly about for an explanation that wouldn't give the game away. "I'm looking for pixies," he said quickly, making it up as he went along. "I hear they hide under stones. I thought—"

"Pixies!" the troll roared.

Kenneth felt his face go pale. The troll had seen

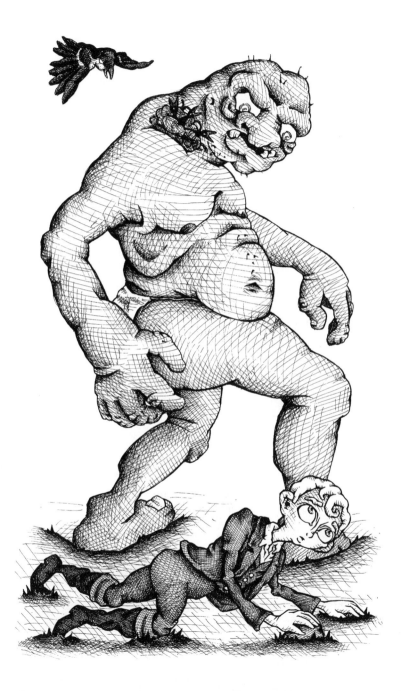

through his lie. "That's what my sister told me," he answered in a small voice.

"And 'ow would thy sister know about pixies?" the troll asked.

"She's a creature catcher, like my uncle," Kenneth answered. His hand was firmly gripping the rock. If the troll would just let go, Kenneth might still catch it off guard with a quick, solid throw. "She's off catching pixies, right now."

The troll's forehead scrunched into a frown. "They be catchin' the lass, as like," it rumbled. It stared off into the distance, as if contemplating something. Slowly.

Kenneth felt the troll's hand lift from his. Quick as a snake, he rolled over and whipped his hand forward, hurling the stone. Unfortunately, it completely missed the troll's head. It glanced off the troll's shoulder instead, snapping a twig off the sparrow's nest. The fledglings inside it peeked out, let out startled cheeps, then disappeared from sight.

The trolls' eyes bulged. "Why, ye little—"

Kenneth barely managed to scramble to his feet before huge hands yanked him into the air. Grumbling ominously, the troll tucked Kenneth under one arm. Tight.

Kenneth, terrified, stayed very, very still.

The troll let out a deep breath, then shook its head. "Bairns," it muttered. "Yon lad, tryin' tae skelp a troll, and a lass, mullockin' about wi' pixies. Silly sods, the both of them." It took another deep, rumbling breath.

Then it nodded, as if it had reached a decision. "Reet, then."

It cupped its free hand around the nest on its shoulder, then began to run.

Kenneth, tucked under its arm, was jostled about like a sack. This time, he really was going to be sick. The troll's elbow dug into his stomach and the ground lurched past with each of its thundering steps. For what seemed an eternity Kenneth was bounced around, unable to catch a solid glimpse of his surroundings as he fought against the desperate need to throw up. At last, thank heavens, the troll slowed to a walk.

"Aye," it rumbled. "As I thowt."

Kenneth twisted his head to see what the troll was looking at. He saw Candace, standing in front of a tumbled cottage, surrounded by a dozen green-skinned creatures no taller than her boots. Pixies. She was bent over at the waist, each hand firmly gripping that of a pixie, turning them around in a slow circle. Dancing with them.

"Candace!" Kenneth called out. "Run back to the dirigible. Fetch Uncle Nigel! Quick!"

Candace ignored him. She didn't even look up.

Kenneth struggled to free himself, but couldn't. The troll's arm was as impossible to bend as an iron bar.

"Candace!" he shouted, angry now. Couldn't she see he was about to be eaten? It looked as though she was going to dance back to the dirigible with the two pixies she'd captured and leave him to his fate. "Stop . . . bloody . . . dancing!" he cried.

Candace at last looked up. She seemed surprised to

see a troll standing a short distance from her, holding her brother under one arm. "Kenneth," she panted. "You've befriended a troll! Tell it—" She seemed out of breath. "To put you down. Come here and—" she panted again. "Help me."

Kenneth ground his teeth in frustration. He couldn't believe his ears. Candace wanted him to help her gather pixies? Candace was stupid, indeed, if she couldn't see that the troll had captured him, not the other way around.

"Yon lass is jiggered," the troll said in a low voice.

"I'll say," Kenneth agreed, thinking it must be yet another word for stupid. The troll seemed to have a lot of those.

"She's near fit tae be eaten," it rumbled.

Kenneth glared at his sister. Then he glanced slyly up at the troll. He'd just thought of a way to get the troll to put him down. "Yes, she is, isn't she?" he said. "Why don't you eat her, then?"

The troll's eyes widened.

"You heard me," Kenneth said. "Eat her, instead of me."

"Thy sister?" the troll asked.

"Yes."

Kenneth pretended to scowl at his sister, as if he loathed her. It wasn't hard. As soon as the troll set him down to grab her, Kenneth would run back to the dirigible. He'd yell at Candace to do the same. If she didn't, and got caught by the troll, Kenneth could at least run back to Uncle Nigel and tell him what had happened.

The troll thought about Kenneth's offer. "Reet, then," it said.

It stepped over something—red-capped mushrooms, Kenneth saw—and walked with great, earth-shaking footsteps toward where Candace was dancing. The pixies squeaked as it approached, and the two who were dancing with Candace wrenched their hands out of hers. They scattered like frightened chickens.

Candace sank down onto a nearby stone, panting. Her hair was damp, her face shiny with sweat. The troll set Kenneth down next to her, but kept a firm hand on his shoulder.

The mother sparrow came back again; she had followed the troll all this way and was once again trying to feed her young. The fledglings cheeped hungrily from the nest on the troll's shoulder. The troll grimaced and clapped a hand against its right ear to block out the sound.

Candace at last caught her breath and glared at Kenneth. "You might have come sooner," she said crossly. She bent over and began unbuttoning her boots.

The tiny green creatures crowded closer. The troll stomped a foot. Several scuttled away to hide in cracks in the ruined cottage, but one of them stood his ground, leaning on a stick with his head cocked. Listening.

"I was in *danger*," Kenneth said hotly. "You were just playing about. *Dancing*. Having fun."

Tiny heads peeped out of the ruined cottage. Yellow eyes watched.

Candace's face reddened with outrage. "Having

fun?" she sputtered. She pulled off her boots and held up a foot. Her sock was spotted with blood. "Look at these blisters! You try dancing for as long as I just did and see how much 'fun' it is."

"Well, it's better than being dragged about by a great hungry troll," Kenneth spat back. "Why don't you try that?"

"Perhaps I will," she spat back. "At least he could carry me."

The pixie leaning on his stick looked up at Candace. "The boy will take your place, then?" he asked in a tiny voice.

"Yes," Candace said, standing up and smoothing out her skirt. "Yes, he will." She turned to the troll. "I'll go with you."

Anger blazed in Kenneth. "Fine," he told his sister. "I'll stay here and dance, and you go and be eaten."

The pixies' eyes gleamed.

"Reet, then," the troll said. Releasing Kenneth, it scooped Candace up. Even as Kenneth opened his mouth to shout at her to run, it tucked her under its arm and strode away. As it did, Candace glanced back over its shoulder at her brother. "Kenneth," she said. "Don't—"

The troll shifted her under its arm, squeezing off the rest of what she'd been about to say.

Kenneth stood, a cold feeling settling into his stomach. He hadn't intended for the troll to actually get hold of Candace. She didn't know how to fight, and she threw stones like a girl. She wouldn't stand a chance of escaping.

"Wait!" Kenneth shouted as the troll lumbered away. "I didn't mean it! Bring her back!"

He tried to run after the troll, but somehow he got turned around and found himself running in a wide circle around the ruined cottage, instead. Being carried by the troll must have left him dizzy. He halted, turned around, and tried again, but once more found himself curving in a circle. Try as many times as he might, he couldn't run in a straight line. He kept circling back to the ruined cottage. It felt almost as if the earth itself were curving underfoot, sending him back to the pixies.

Wizened green faces peeked out from between the stones of the ruined cottage, their yellow eyes gleaming. The pixies climbed out of their hiding places among the rocks and picked up sticks with sharpened points. They advanced on Kenneth like a horde of tiny warriors.

"Dance!" they squeaked, poking his ankles. "Dance."

Kenneth gulped.

Candace stared at her brother as the troll carried her away, suddenly feeling sorry. What had she just done? Kenneth had made her cross, but did he really deserve to be left with pixies, to dance with them until his feet were blistered? Candace herself would eventually have talked them into letting her leave their circle, she was certain of that. But Kenneth was all bluster and fight. He'd only anger them, and then they'd *never* let him go.

A tear trickled down her cheek, but she didn't have a hand free to wipe it away. She snuffled.

The troll shifted her into the crook of his arm so that she was cradled against his broad chest. "Why are ye cryin', lass?" he asked.

Candace looked up into eyes round and glassy as marbles. "Because of Kenneth," she said.

The troll glanced over his shoulder. "Tha' scraumy little nobbut?" he rumbled. "Think on this, lass: he was happy tae send thee tae thy death."

"What do you mean?" Candace asked, genuinely puzzled.

The troll bared his teeth. "Yon lad hoped I would eat thee."

"Nonsense," Candace replied. "You aren't going to hurt me."

"Oh, aye?" he growled. "What makes thee sae sure?"

Candace pointed at the nest on its shoulder. "The sparrows," she told it. "I can see how their cheeping irritates you, yet you haven't knocked their nest from your shoulder. And when their mother came around, you could have swatted her like a mosquito with those great big hands of yours. You didn't."

The troll set Candace down on the ground and loomed over her. "Trolls *eat* bairns," it thundered.

Candace shrugged. "No, you don't. If you did, you'd have eaten my brother. You're only trying to look gruff, to frighten people away."

"Humans," the troll said. "'Tis humans that vexes me. Muckin' about and diggin' up the best peat, afore I gets a chance tae scup it."

Candace nodded, even though she had no idea what the troll was talking about. "I imagine that would be annoying," she agreed. "There's one thing I don't understand, though."

"Aye?" the troll asked suspiciously.

"If those sparrows irritate you so, why don't you take the nest from your shoulder and lay it on the ground? You could do it gently, so as not to hurt them."

The troll shook his head slowly. "'Tis nae possible."

"Why not?"

"Yon pixies," he said with a frown. "The moors is thick with 'em. They'd cadger the spuggies right out of the nest, soon as I were tae trundle away."

"What would pixies want with sparrows?"

"They eats 'em. There's nowt as pixies likes better than the taste of a spuggie."

"I see," Candace said. She looked about the moors. She could see the troll's point. Even if he were to set the nest down on a high rock, the pixies would clamber up to it in a flash. "The point remains, the part about you eating me is nonsense. Just look at how you befriended my brother."

The troll's eyes narrowed. "I would nae call it that, as such." He shrugged. Gently, so the sparrows wouldn't be disturbed. "Yon lad didnae even tell me his name."

"He was afraid of you," Candace told him. "But I'm not." She curtseyed. "Candace Owen. And you are—?"

The troll took a deep breath. "Rumblegut."

What an odd name, Candace thought. But it wouldn't be polite to comment on it. She supposed it was because of the sound his stomach was making, like rocks in a tumbler. It sounded as though the troll were constantly hungry.

"Pleased to meet you, Master Rumblegut," she said, curtseying a second time. She glanced around and saw that the ruined cottage was already far behind them. Too far to see what was happening to Kenneth. She turned back to the troll. "Now, if you would be so kind, Rumblegut, as to take me back to the pixies so that I can fetch my brother?"

"No."

Candace frowned. "Why ever not?"

"He has joined their dance. 'Tis faerie magic at work there. The dancer cannae stop caperin' about 'til yon pixies give him leave."

"Well, I'll just ask them to let him go, then."

Another head shake. "Nae, lass. They will nae let him go. They never do. Yon pixies will dance thy brother until he drops. And then——"

Candace felt her eyes widen. She thought of the skull in the ruined cottage. She'd convinced herself that the poor departed soul must have died in the collapse of his cottage, and not because of anything the pixies had done, but now she wasn't so sure.

"And then?" she whispered.

The troll stared across the moors. "The pixies will nae let the bairn go unless some other takes his place.

Some other that be willin'. Nae one 'round here be foolish enough tae do that."

Candace stamped her foot—and immediately regretted it. Those blisters *hurt*. "Then why did you leave him there?"

The troll stared down at her. "Not I, lass, but thee. T'was thee as struck a bargain wi' yon pixies. Thee gave them Kenneth in return for thine own freedom."

Candace took a deep breath, struggling to maintain her poise. Guilty tears prickled at the corners of her eyes. She reached in her pocket for a hankie, then remembered that the pixies had torn it up.

She stared up at Rumblegut. To a pixie, he'd look even more enormous than he did to her. "The pixies are frightened of you," she said. "Can't you just go and take Kenneth from them?"

The troll shook his head. "If t'were only that simple," he said. "But I can nae more carry him out of that faerie ring than I can pluck the sun from the sky. Even were I tae drive the pixies away, yon Kenneth would remain where he's at, inside o' that ring. Dancing 'til the end o' his days."

"I see," Candace said in a hushed voice. This was bad. Very bad.

Her eye fell on the dirigible, a small white lump in the distance. Certainly, she thought, Uncle Nigel would know what to do. Pixies, he'd said, had been "well documented" by the Royal Cryptozoological Society. They must have some known weakness—something, other than cream and handkerchiefs, that they were fond of that could be bartered in exchange for Kenneth. The only trouble was, Candace would never be able to walk as far as the dirigible on blistered feet. She held her boots, but winced at the thought of putting them on again. Her feet were throbbing.

"My uncle will know what to do," she told Rumblegut. She pointed at the dirigible. "He's over there. Please, would you take me to him?"

Rumblegut scratched the skin around the nest with a finger. He looked uneasy. "Thine uncle be a creature catcher," he said. "Wi' chains. I'll nae go anywhere near him."

"But I need you to carry me!" Candace begged.

Rumblegut started to move away. "I'll take my leave of thee now, lass," he told her over his shoulder. "Fare thee well."

"Wait!" Candace cried, stumbling after him on her blistered feet. She grabbed the troll's hand before he could walk away. Or rather, grabbed a finger; his hand was very big.

"Catching a troll was entirely Kenneth's idea," she told the troll. "And a blessed foolish notion, I might add. Uncle Nigel has absolutely no interest in trolls. None whatsoever. He came to the Moorlands to catch a will o' the wisp."

The troll's eyebrows raised. "Oh, aye?"

"Yes. Absolutely no interest in trolls at all." Candace pointed at the troll's feet, which had sunk into the soft peat as he'd stood talking to her. "You're far too big and heavy; you'd only weigh the dirigible down; we'd never get off the ground."

The troll stared thoughtfully at the dirigible, then returned its attention to Candace. "A will o' the wisp, ye say?"

"Yes, that's right," Candace said, clinging to the troll's hand.

"Thine uncle should nae muck about wi' those."

"What do you mean?" Candace asked.

The troll's expression was grim. "Will o' the wisps be the souls of the dead. Of them as drowns in bogs."

"They're not marsh gas, then?"

The troll chuckled. "Nae, lass. Much more dangerous than that. They be angry. Restless. If ye riles 'em, thee like as nowt will wind up a will o' the wisp thyself."

Candace felt a chill run down her spine, as if someone had just walked across the ground that would one day be her grave. "What do you mean?"

"A will o' the wisp will lead ye tae deep water, where thee drowns," the troll said in an ominous voice. "A fate that may have befallen thine uncle."

"Nonsense," she said in her bravest voice. "Even if he did fall into deep water, Uncle Nigel's a strong swimmer. And he knows what he's doing. I'm certain he knows everything there is to know about will o' the wisps."

Rumblegut said nothing.

"Please," Candace begged, laying her cheek against the troll's broad hand. It felt cold and hard as stone—

something she hoped his heart wasn't. "If will o' the wisps are truly that dangerous, I need to find my uncle before he tries to capture one," she told the troll. "If what you said is true and he does disappear, there will be no one left to rescue Kenneth. I'll be all alone. Please, won't you at least carry me back to the dirigible?"

She looked up at the troll, this time letting the tears flow. She had confidence in Uncle Nigel; he'd been on dozens of expeditions to far more dangerous places than the Moorlands. He wasn't going to run afoul of a little ball of light. But if she was going to get back to the dirigible in time to rescue Kenneth before he dropped from exhaustion, she needed the troll's help.

Rumblegut gave a heavy sigh that sounded like wind whistling from a cave. He squatted and extended his arms. "Climb up, lass," he said. "I'll take ye as far as yon dirigible. But one glimpse of thine uncle, and I'll be setting thee down and skitterin' away."

6

Kenneth glared at the pixies. He'd already discovered he couldn't leave on his own accord. He'd have to fight his way out. He managed to stomp one foot the way the troll had, but the pixies didn't scatter. Perhaps they were too stupid to realize that he meant business.

"It's a fight you want, then, is it?" he told them. "Right."

The pixies were tiny creatures—they looked ridiculous with those little spears. Kenneth raised his fists in the guard position, then realized that to punch the pixies he'd have to either get down on his knees or bend double at the waist. Not a very dignified way to box.

The pixies jabbed his ankles with the points of their spears. "Dance!" they yelled.

Kenneth kicked the nearest pixie. Or rather, he tried to. In mid-kick his foot twisted to the side, all on its own, as if he'd intended a sweeping step to the right. He tried to kick again, this time with his left foot, and once more missed his target entirely. His kick went high, he lost his balance, and he wound up flat on his back.

The pixies laughed.

Kenneth scrambled upright again, but it did little good. Compelled by pixie magic, his feet at first shuffled, then broke into a dance. By concentrating fiercely, Kenneth dodged the pixies' spear thrusts. He raised his fists again in a boxer's pose.

When they weren't expecting it, he punched down. The pixie he'd aimed at danced aside, however, and Kenneth's fist grazed a stone. Ouch! Wincing, he shook away the pain.

The pixies laughed.

He punched again. Missed again, his fist slamming down into soft peat.

His feet kept dancing.

Kenneth eyed his foes. He couldn't fathom why Candace had wanted to capture one. They'd be about as decorative in her garden as a lump of coal. Their faces were the color of overcooked peas and equally unpleasant to contemplate, with their hideous wrinkles, leering mouths, and odd yellow eyes. Kenneth had never seen anything nastier. Except, perhaps, Mrs. Soames's face when she'd shouted at Kenneth for "upsetting" her stupid little dog.

The pixies squeaked like rats and kept poking his ankles with their sticks. Some of them were clearly female, but equally as vicious as the males. If Kenneth did manage to punch one, he certainly wouldn't feel sorry for it.

His punches, however, weren't coming anywhere near the mark. Bending over and driving his fist down toward the ground was too awkward, and the pixies were simply too quick for him. Two of them ran at him, holding either end of a stick. Kenneth's feet danced him straight into it and he tripped. He fell face down on the ground and was instantly surrounded by squealing pixies.

"Clumsy boy, clumsy boy!" they taunted. Kenneth rolled away from them, his legs flailing as if they were dancing.

"On your feet!" they shrilled. "Dance."

Kenneth spat out peat and gave them a furious glare as he rose to his knees. He fished his knife out of his pocket and unfolded it, intending to scare them away by waving it at them, but one of the pixies smacked it out of his hands with its stick. Kenneth scrambled after his knife, trying to grab it, but his traitorous legs forced him upright and danced him away from it. The open blade glinted against the dark ground. One of the pixies ran over to the knife and picked it up.

"Shall we dance him over to the willies?" one of the pixies asked the others. "It's easier if we do it that way."

"No," the one holding the knife answered. "They don't need another. We'll finish him up right here."

Kenneth steeled himself. "So you want to play rough, do you?" he gritted as manfully as he could. His voice, however, had a quiver in it. This wasn't like facing the boys at school. They might be bigger than Kenneth, but no matter how fierce their taunts, they'd stop after giving him a bloody nose.

These pixies meant to dance him to death. He'd

wind up a skeleton out here on the lonely moors, like the one he'd just glimpsed inside the pile of stones that was the ruined cottage.

He smiled. Stones.

Weaving his way through them toward the ruined cottage, Kenneth suddenly bent and picked up a stone. He hurled it at the nearest pixie. The rock crashed into it, sending it tumbling.

Kenneth cheered.

A sharp pain flared in his ankle. He looked down and saw that a pixie had just stabbed him with his own knife! Distracted, he hadn't noticed it circling around behind him.

"Thundering damnation!" he cried. An adult oath. One an eleven-year-old boy wasn't supposed to know, let alone use. But if Kenneth didn't work quickly, he wouldn't live to see twelve, let alone learn any new oaths.

Scrabbling at the ruined cottage, he managed to pick up a stone in each hand. He hurled one, then the other. Too hastily—one throw went wide and his second target dodged neatly aside.

The pixies squeaked at each other. As Kenneth lunged for two more rocks, they dove for cover, disappearing once more into cracks between the stones. Kenneth's feet danced him away from their hiding places, around to the far side of the ruined cottage. Laughter came from the heap of stones.

Furious, Kenneth hurled one of his missiles at a face that peeped out. The pixie ducked. The stone glanced off the pile and arced away into the air, landing with a thud some distance behind the ruin.

Abruptly, the laughter stopped. So did Kenneth's dancing feet.

He paused, his second stone raised. He'd just accomplished—something. But what?

He took a cautious step toward the ruin, intent upon seeing what the pixies were up to. They were moving about in there. Then one of them suddenly bolted from the ruin. He saw it abruptly stop, then run back and forth, continuously crossing the same small patch of ground. It was running between the mushrooms the troll had stepped over earlier—the ones that grew in a ring around the ruined cottage, several paces from it.

The mushroom ring that Kenneth's stone had just smashed a hole through.

"That's it," Kenneth whispered. "The way out."

The break slowly mended itself as tiny—but rapidly growing—mushrooms sprang up where the pixie had run back and forth. Kenneth started toward it. A pixie ran between his legs and spat on his boot, then darted away. He ignored it. Then the rest of the pixies emerged from their hiding places and rushed Kenneth in a wave. Sticks cracked against his ankles, sending him staggering. Kenneth stomped, narrowly missing one of the pixies, and the rest scattered—only to rush back at him. He stomped again, then kicked. They ran. He chased after them. He'd teach these little blighters a lesson, by thunder.

The pixies laughed and raced around the side of the ruined cottage.

Kenneth followed, then abruptly halted as he realized what the pixies were trying to do. Leading him in a circle around the ruined cottage—something that would start him dancing again. Meanwhile, the mushroom ring was repairing itself. And once it did, Kenneth would be trapped inside.

He turned and bolted for the hole instead. In just a few strides, he was there. Sensing the invisible barrier before he came to it, he twisted his body sideways, like a rugby player trying to squeeze through two defenders, and burst through the gap in the ring. As he ran, he glanced over his shoulder. The pixies had slowed to a halt and were shaking their fists at him. One of them screamed with rage and hurled its spear, but the tiny weapon fell far short.

Kenneth skidded to a halt on the soft peat and made a rude gesture—one he'd seen an Italian peddler use once behind Daisy's back when she refused to buy his bruised apples. A flick of the fingers against the chin. Kenneth didn't know what it meant—he only knew that it was something nasty.

As nasty as pixies. None of which seemed inclined to leave their mushroom ring, or to follow him.

Kenneth turned and hurried in the direction the troll had gone.

He hoped he wasn't too late to rescue Candace.

As it was carrying Candace back to the dirigible, the troll paused to look down at something on the ground. Glancing down, Candace saw it was a shirt, muddy and wet. "Why, that's Old Tom's," she exclaimed. "He must have run this way."

"Old Tom?" Rumblegut said. "And who would he be? Thy dog?"

"No, silly," Candace replied. "He's one of my uncle's servants."

"Human?"

"Of course."

The troll pointed at the ground with a thick finger. "These be wolf prints."

He was right. All around the shirt were small, roundish footprints, like those left by a dog. Candace remembered the howl she'd heard the night before, and shivered.

"Do you think the wolves were chasing Old Tom?" she asked. "Do you think they . . . caught him?" She pictured great snarling beasts, tearing Old Tom's shirt clean off his back.

The troll bent and picked the shirt up. "'Tain't torn," he observed, holding it up so Candace could see that it had been unbuttoned. He walked a few steps farther, moving toward the dirigible. "These be a man's footprints, here."

Candace looked again. Rumblegut was right; the soft ground held prints well, and she could see where human footprints left off and those of a wolf began. A faint suspicion started to dawn. "You mean—?" she began.

"Aye," Rumblegut said. "Old Tom be nowt but a shifter."

"A . . . shifter?" Candace asked. "You mean a lycanthrope, don't you?" Suddenly, the reason behind Old Tom leaving the dirigible became clear. He'd been glancing toward the east in anticipation of the moonrise. When it had come, he'd run off, rather than shift into a wolf in the confines of the gondola. She admired Old Tom for doing the noble thing: removing himself before he became a brutish wolf that would terrify the children he was meant to be keeping watch over.

"Poor fellow," Candace breathed.

"Aye," Rumblegut agreed. "He be a wolf but one moon a month, and a man the rest."

Candace nodded politely, even though she didn't see what was so bad about that. Who would want to run around as a howling beast all the time? Imagine the fleas. She couldn't quite picture Old Tom as a lycanthrope, however. He'd seemed so . . . normal.

She glanced up at the sun. It was high overhead—midday already. And she hadn't eaten anything since last night. Her stomach growled with hunger, a most unladylike sound. "We should be getting along," she told Rumblegut.

The troll gave a slight shrug that started the fledglings cheeping again. He dropped the muddy shirt and continued on his way.

As he walked, Rumblegut shifted Candace from one arm to the other. "Lass," he said, "might I ask thee summat?"

"Of course," Candace said.

"Why were thee muckin' about wi' pixies for, anywise?"

"I was collecting them for the contest."

"What contest might that be?"

"The one sponsored by the *Londinium Times*," Candace answered. "There's a prize for the child who collects the most unusual creature."

The troll thought about this. "And when yon contest be over and done?"

"What do you mean?"

"The creatures," Rumblegut said. "What of them? Where will they go, an' all?"

"Well, some of them will wind up in the zoo, I should think," Candace answered. "Or in the museum, if they're d—" She abruptly paused, realizing it might upset Rumblegut to hear that some of the creatures might no longer be living when they were submitted to the contest. That they would wind up being stuffed by a taxidermist and made into exhibits for the museum.

"Whatever creature I catch shall go in my garden," she said.

"What garden might that be?"

"Why, the Lady Candace Owen's Public Gardens," Candace answered. "It won't be built for several years yet. But when it is, it will be the most wonderful garden ever." Warming to the subject, she told Rumblegut all about her great public work. It would be beautiful. A tonic for the working classes. Children would marvel at the creatures she would stock its grounds with. "The creatures would be free to roam wherever they wished," she added. "Within the gardens, of course."

"And if they try tae leave—tae trundle off home again?" Rumblegut asked.

Candace frowned. "Leave?" she said. "Whatever for? The gardens would be their home. They'd be happy there, and well cared for."

"Oh, aye. But if yon creatures wanted tae go?"

"They wouldn't," Candace insisted. "They *couldn't*. They'd be an essential part of the gardens. Without fairies fluttering among the nasturtiums, and winter deer to turn the fountain spray to ice, and pegasi for the children to ride, it would just be another garden, like every other one in the city."

The troll said nothing for several moments. "This garden of thine . . . it be a cage, then."

"No!" Candace protested. Rumblegut wasn't understanding this at all. "It will be a tribute to beauty and nature. A lasting monument to the harmony that can exist between man and beast. A place where—"

"Why do thee need a monument?" the troll rumbled.

"It's not for me," Candace said, slightly exasperated now. "The Lady Candace Owen's Public Gardens will be for the children of Londinium. And for their children. And for their—"

"Like as nowt to call it Bairns Gardens, then."

"But I'm the one who will build it!"

Rumblegut chuckled. "What—all by thyself?"

"No, silly. Workmen will do it."

"Ah," the troll said. He thought a moment. "Workmen's Gardens, then."

"Oh!" Candace exclaimed. "You've not been listening. It's to be named after me since I'm the benefactor. It's to be a charitable work, for the public good."

"Nae for the good of yon creatures in it?"

"You haven't been *listening*," Candace said. "They'll be well cared for. And some are on the verge of extinction. If they're not collected, the last of the species will die out."

"Will thee ask if they want tae live in the garden?"

"Ask?" Candace echoed.

"Aye, ask."

"Fine," Candace snapped. "Rumblegut, would you like to live in my garden?"

The troll grinned. His quartz teeth sparkled in the sunlight. "Aye."

"You see?" Candace cried. "You—" She blinked in surprise. "You would?"

"Aye. 'Twould be a lark tae see yon bairns gawping when I open me gob and roor at 'em. But I would nae come if I could nae leave as it pleased me."

"I see," Candace said. "Well then, I suppose it's all arranged." She was being sarcastic, of course. She didn't want a great roaring troll in her gardens.

But she did see his point. If creatures came willingly to her garden—if they didn't need to be captured—it would save her a lot of bother. And the creatures themselves would be happier. But they couldn't expect to go traipsing off whenever they pleased. Even servants only got a half day off a week, and they were human. Creatures could hardly expect more.

Rumblegut kept walking.

As they drew closer to the dirigible, Candace could see a knot of men standing beside it. One of them was gesturing as if directing the others to do something. Seeing them, the troll slowed, then stopped.

"Nae farther," he rumbled, his glasslike eyes locked on the gesturing man. "The catcher's there." He set Candace down.

The man who was gesturing was shorter than the rest. Even from this distance, Candace could see that he had gray hair and sideburns. "That's not my uncle," she told Rumblegut. "It's Old Tom."

"Aye? And yon others?"

"They're the peat cutters," Candace said. "No threat to you at all. They're simply here to hold the lines as the dirigible launches." Behind the dirigible, she could just make out the pony and its cart. Uncle Nigel must have returned. He would be inside the gondola, stowing his equipment away.

The peat cutters began pointing in Candace's direction. They'd spotted her and the troll. Old Tom broke away from them at a run, waving to the peat cutters to follow him. A handful of them scooped up crescent-bladed spades and trotted in his wake, but the others hung back, exchanging uneasy glances.

Rumblegut backed away as they approached.

"Wait!" Candace implored. "Please don't go."

The troll glanced back and forth between Candace and Old Tom, who had sprinted out ahead of the peat cutters and was approaching fast. "Why?" he asked.

"Because . . . well, because I don't want you to go yet. I like you."

The troll nodded at the approaching humans. "They don't."

Candace glanced at Old Tom and the peat cutters. "It's all right," she shouted. "The troll doesn't mean me any harm. He's my friend."

The peat cutters who had followed Old Tom slowed, lowered their spades slightly. Old Tom kept on running, however.

"Does yon shifter mean me harm?" Rumblegut asked.

"Oh no," Candace said quickly. "It's me he's cross with. Last night, Kenneth and I were supposed to stay in the dirigible. Uncle Nigel told Old Tom to watch us, but we managed to sneak away. He likely received a stern reprimand this morning."

The troll considered this. "I'll abide a little wi' thee," he told Candace. "But I'll nae go any closer to yon dirigible."

Old Tom skidded to a stop a short distance from Candace. "*Fraulein!*" he cried in a relieved voice. "You have returned." He glanced hopefully around. "And your brother? *Wo ist*—?" He paused abruptly, and pointed a finger at the troll. "You! What have you done with the boy?"

"Ye've nae cause tae be vexed with me, shifter," the troll rumbled back in an ominously low voice.

Old Tom's eyes widened. "Shifter? You are mistaken. I am not—"

"It's all right, Tom," Candace reassured him. "I already know you're a lycanthrope."

Old Tom gave her a startled look.

"And you needn't be cross with Rumblegut. He saved me from the pixies after I got caught in their faerie ring. They were dancing me to exhaustion. You see?" She lifted a blistered foot.

Old Tom's eyes widened.

Rumblegut moved closer. "Yon pixies has the second bairn now. He be in a right fix with them. Yon lass said as nowt but their uncle could help. I fetched her back, even tho' that uncle be a catcher."

Old Tom's worried frown deepened. "The pixies have Herr Kenneth?"

"Uncle Nigel will know what to do, Tom," Candace reassured him. "He'll know how to rescue my brother."

The peat cutters approached, spades loosely gripped in their hands. Candace motioned for them to lower their tools.

"It's all right," she told them. "Rumblegut won't hurt you." She gripped the troll's massive hand. "You see? He's a sweet-tempered troll."

Rumblegut grinned.

The peat cutters jumped back.

"Don't smile," Candace hissed. "You're scaring them."

Rumblegut closed his mouth.

The peat cutters relaxed. A little.

Old Tom swept his cap from his head. He turned it around in his hands with quick, nervous gestures. "Unfortunately your uncle has not returned, *fraulein*. I am . . . concerned. One of the peat cutters found the pony this morning, wandering across the moors with its cart. No one was aboard it."

"Aye," said one of the peat cutters—a heavyset man in muddy gumboots. "There was no trace of Master Owen."

Candace felt a sliver of worry. "Do you think Uncle Nigel fell off the cart on his way back to the dirigible? Could he be injured and lying on the moors?"

The man in gumboots nodded gloomily, but Old Tom shook his head. "I think not, *fraulein*, for the cart was not loaded. Had your uncle been returning on it, so too would his equipment be on board it."

Candace's sliver of worry became a cold wedge of fear. Perhaps Rumblegut had been right. Perhaps Uncle Nigel had been led away by the will o' the wisps.

No, Candace thought firmly, forcing that thought from her mind. The pony had probably just been spooked by something—maybe even Old Tom as he was tearing about in wolf form last night. It had bolted, leaving Uncle Nigel to trudge back on his own.

"Well, we'll just have to look for him, then," she said, putting a cheerful tone in her voice. "Won't we?"

Old Tom gave a quick, nervous smile. "*Ja, fraulein*. I was organizing the search, even as you approached. We will follow the cart tracks back to their starting point, and search from there. Gott willing, we will soon find Herr Owen and all will be well."

Candace nodded. Uncle Nigel would be located and brought back to the dirigible. She had no doubt about that. But Kenneth had yet to be saved.

Beside her, however, Rumblegut was slowly shaking his head.

7

Kenneth was surprised to see the troll's footprints leading in the direction of the dirigible. He couldn't imagine why it had headed there. Unless, of course, it had finished with Candace and found itself hungry for more. Perhaps, even now, it was doing battle with Uncle Nigel. He could picture the scene in his mind: the troll, looming large, battering its way into the gondola with great sledgehammer fists. Uncle Nigel, inside, standing up to the beast with bravado alone. Or perhaps with a smoking pistol in one hand. Or an elephant gun.

Kenneth broke into a run.

As he drew closer to the dirigible, he could see that its gondola was undamaged. Uncle Nigel must have managed to drive the troll away. But what of Candace? Kenneth would know in another moment. Already he had reached the enormous shadow cast by the gas bag. He thought he could hear his sister's voice, coming from the other side of the gondola. A faint laugh:

Candace, putting up a brave face, despite the grievous wounds she'd suffered at the hands of the troll.

Kenneth rounded the corner of the gondola and skidded to a halt. Instead of the scene of carnage he'd expected, he saw his sister and the troll sitting down to tea together. Candace was seated on a folding chair, eating a sandwich, her feet wrapped in bandages, while the troll sat on the ground, its bottom sunk into the soft peat. A folding table laden with sandwiches and a thermos of tea stood between them. The troll held a teacup in one massive hand; with its other hand it scooped up a handful of peat and popped this into its mouth. It chewed. Noisily. Then washed the mouthful down with a gulp of tea. For several seconds, all Kenneth could do was stand and gape.

Candace spotted him and sat bolt upright on her chair. "Kenneth!"

Kenneth looked around for Uncle Nigel and Old Tom, but didn't see either of them. Candace seemed to be alone with the troll, which she'd obviously intimidated into not eating her. "What . . . what are you doing?" he asked tentatively.

The troll gave a wicked grin. "We're suppin'," it rumbled. It held up its cup. "Young Kenneth, would ye fancy some tea? Ye must be thirsty after all that dancing."

Candace rose to her feet and shuffled toward Kenneth. Judging by the amazed look on her face, she'd never expected to see him again. "Kenneth," she said again. "How ever did you talk the pixies into letting you go?"

CREATURE CATCHERS

Kenneth took a deep breath, then grinned. "I didn't *talk* the pixies into letting me go. I used rocks. I threw one and broke a hole through their mushroom ring, and then drove the pixies back with a hail of stones."

He expected Candace to look horrified and say something stupid like, "Oh, those poor little dears!" or one of her usual remarks. Instead, she quietly nodded.

"Those pixies," Kenneth added ominously, "were going to kill me."

"Aye," the troll rumbled softly. "Like as nowt."

"But instead of coming back to help me," Kenneth accused, "you just sat around here at the dirigible. Having *tea*."

Candace's face reddened. "I came back to fetch Uncle Nigel, but he wasn't here. Old Tom and the peat cutters are out looking for him now. Once they found him, I was going to send him to save you, straight away. There was time, yet. You could have lasted a long time, dancing."

"Those pixies weren't content to just dance," Kenneth retorted. "They were fierce as Gurkhas. They cut me with my own pocketknife. Just look." He hiked up his trouser leg.

Candace barely glanced at the wound on his ankle. "You got away."

Kenneth glared. "You knew those pixies were dangerous, but you left me there. You *wanted* them to hurt me."

"Well, you gave me to the troll," Candace snapped. "You wanted him to *eat* me."

"Say you're sorry!" Kenneth insisted.

"No." Candace leaned uncomfortably close. "*You* say you're sorry."

Kenneth balled his fists. He was practically eyeball to eyeball with her now. "No."

"Say it."

"No. You say it."

"No."

The troll rose to its feet, slowly shaking its head. "Worse'n spuggies," it grumbled.

Kenneth leaned even closer to Candace. "You apologize first," he said in a fierce whisper.

"I won't!" Candace stomped on his foot, then immediately winced.

Kenneth smirked. "Go on," he taunted. "Try it again, why don't y—"

A heavy hand thumped down on Kenneth's shoulder. Another descended on Candace's. The troll pulled them apart. It leaned down over Kenneth and bared jagged teeth. "Stop moithering yon lass right now, or ye'll be sorry."

Kenneth shrank back.

Candace sighed. "Oh, Rumblegut, stop. Kenneth's no more frightened of you than I am. Isn't that right, Kenneth?"

Kenneth gulped. "That's right," he said. He squared his shoulders and met the troll's eye with a nonchalant, devil-may-care look his uncle would have been proud of. Then he turned to Candace. "So where do you think Uncle Nigel is?"

"The peat cutters think he may be out by the bog," Candace said. "That's where they're searching. Old Tom is with them, and he's certain Uncle Nigel will turn up safe and sound, but—" Her voice dropped to a nervous whisper. "Rumblegut thinks the will o' the wisps led him away to drown."

Then she smiled brightly, although the smile looked false. "That's nonsense, of course. Uncle Nigel can take care of himself."

"Uncle Nigel's in danger?" Kenneth asked incredulously. "Then why aren't you out looking for him too?"

"Because of my blisters," she retorted, holding up one bandage-wrapped foot. "I can barely walk."

Kenneth glanced up at the gas bag that loomed over them. "Why didn't you use the dirigible to search for him?"

"I thought of that, but Old Tom didn't how to fly it. Nor do I."

"I do," Kenneth said.

Candace rolled her eyes. Her brother had held the wheel for a few moments, and now he thought he was a dirigible pilot. Typical. "And where would you fly it to, exactly, Kenneth? You haven't got a clue as to where Uncle Nigel might have gone. The peat cutters, on the other hand, know the moors. They'll find Uncle Nigel." She paused, her attention caught by something in the distance. "You see? There they are now. They're returning."

Kenneth looked in the direction she was pointing and saw the peat cutters returning with the pony cart. As it drew closer, he could see Old Tom sitting on it, holding the reins, but no sign of Uncle Nigel. Kenneth hurried toward it. Behind him, the troll scooped up Candace and followed with slow, lumbering steps, carrying her. The sight gave Kenneth a momentary pang of fear, but Candace seemed quite comfortable in the troll's arms.

Kenneth reached the cart first.

"Herr Kenneth!" Old Tom cried, relief plain in his voice. "You have returned!"

"Have you found Uncle Nigel?" Kenneth asked.

Old Tom shook his head. "Of your uncle, there was no sign."

"We saw his device," one of the peat cutters said. He was younger than the rest, his lank brown hair combed straight back from a high forehead. One eyebrow was higher than the other; it gave him an odd expression, as if he were angry and astonished at the same time. "On the shore of the bog. It had sunk into the peat, and was leaning and about to fall over, but George straightened it." He scowled, then added, "Despite my warnings, I might add. The device was humming like an infernal chorus and sparking hellfire. The Good Lord never intended for lightning to be in the service of man."

"Lightning?" Kenneth repeated. "You mean electricity?"

The peat cutter nodded grimly. "Lightning is God's thunderbolt, reserved for His use alone."

A few of the other men nodded in agreement.

"We also found your uncle's footprints," Old Tom said. "They led into the bog."

"Into the water," added the man in gumboots.

"In—but not out again. Master Owen must be lying dead at the bottom of the bog."

Kenneth felt a chill slide down his spine.

The troll lumbered up at that moment—causing the peat cutters to all take a step or two back—and deposited Candace on the ground. Her face was pale. She must have heard what had just been said.

Old Tom gave the gloomy peat cutter a stern look. "We do not know what, precisely, has happened to Herr Owen," he said. "He may have exited the bog at some other point. On the far side, perhaps, where we have not yet searched."

"Where is he, then?" another of the men asked—this one, a fellow with a bristling red beard and small, squinty eyes. "The bog's miles across, but 'tis flat as a table. We should have seen him."

"You never see anything, Ned, but what's right in front of your nose," another quipped.

The peat cutters all laughed. All but one.

"He's lost," the man in gumboots said in his mournful voice. "Those that follow the will o' the wisps into the bog are never seen again."

Kenneth felt as if a pit had opened under him. His eyes suddenly began to sting. He glanced at Candace. She too was blinking furiously.

Old Tom clambered off the pony cart and knelt next to them. "There's always hope, *kinder*. Your uncle might yet return." He glanced up at the other peat cutters for confirmation, but none of them met his eye. They all stared at the ground with long faces.

Candace turned to Old Tom. "Thomas! You can find Uncle Nigel by scent."

Old Tom's face paled. "*Fraulein*, please. Do not speak of that." He gave the peat cutters a sidelong glance.

Kenneth frowned. "He can what?"

Candace whispered in his ear. "He's a lycanthrope. He can shift into wolf form. But don't tell anyone."

So that was what had happened to Old Tom last night. Kenneth was surprised. Old Tom looked so small. So much the humble servant. Kenneth was hard pressed to imagine him with a slavering muzzle full of wolf teeth. He wished he'd chased after Old Tom. He would have liked to have seen him shift.

Old Tom stood. "Alas, *fraulein*, my faculties of smell are not always so keen," he told Candace in a quiet voice. "They are a product of the . . . of the evening light, not of the will. And you are forgetting that a scent does not linger on water. Especially if one is . . . below the water."

The hollow feeling returned to Kenneth's stomach.

"Do you really think Uncle Nigel might have drowned, Thomas?" Candace asked in a tight voice.

"Nonsense," Kenneth said in a voice that was braver than he felt. He needed to reassure Candace. Girls could be delicate and emotional creatures. "Uncle Nigel's survived worse. Remember him telling us about the time he was carried off by a hippogriff?"

Candace nodded, no doubt thinking back, like Kenneth, to the row of talon marks in each of Uncle Nigel's shoulders—now healed, but a livid red when he'd first shown them to the children. A hippogriff had carried Uncle Nigel to its nest, intending to tear him up to feed to its young. Uncle Nigel had shown it a gold pocket watch, then hurled the watch down the cliff face. While the hippogriff swooped after the glittering object, Uncle Nigel had scrambled down the other side of the peak and hiked thirty miles back to safety, blood leaking from the punctures in his shoulders all the while.

"Wading around in water isn't going to hurt Uncle Nigel," Kenneth concluded. "Even if he stumbled into a deep spot, he's a strong swimmer. And it's not as though the will o' the wisps could have hurt him; they're just little balls of light."

Despite his reassurances, Candace looked worried.

"'Tis nae just a ball of light," the troll rumbled.

"Oh?" Kenneth turned. "What is it, then?"

"'Tis a soul."

"Yes, well." Kenneth waved his hand. "My point being that it's a non-corporeal creature. It's not as though a will o' the wisp could have held Uncle Nigel's head underwater, or anything."

"It would nae need to. A will o' the wisp has other ways of bringing a man tae grief."

Candace glanced up at the troll, a worried expression on her face. "Is there something you haven't told us, Rumblegut?"

The troll cleared its throat—a sound like stones tumbling in a rock polisher. It seemed reluctant to speak. "Well, lass, there's this. Will o' the wisps dinnae just float about waitin' tae be followed. Yon beasties seize hold of the mind and sap the will. That's as how they lures ye off into the bog, to a deep patch. Them as is captured dinnae even *try* tae swim. They just . . . sink."

Candace's face paled.

"But they's nae truly dead and drowned," the troll added. "The magic of the will o' the wisps sustains their bodies 'til sunset. That's when the soul rises from yon body, a will o' the wisp itself. 'Tis like planting a seed; that's as how will o' the wisps make more—"

"Oh," said Candace in a tight, small voice. She swayed, looking as though she was about to faint.

Kenneth himself felt unsteady and off-kilter. Assuming the troll was right—and Kenneth was starting to realize that it wasn't so stupid, after all—Uncle Nigel was in terrible danger. If he was underwater and they didn't find him by sunset, he'd die.

He glanced up at the dirigible. Perhaps from the air, Uncle Nigel might be spotted. Then Kenneth realized something, and his hopes dimmed. If Uncle Nigel truly had sunk under the water, they'd never be able to spot him. Bog water was dark and murky; trying to see through it would be like peering into a glass of ink.

"We've got to keep searching," Candace said. "But where, exactly? The bog is enormous and Uncle Nigel might have waded some distance from the shore before going under."

Kenneth wracked his brain, searching for a solution.

"Uncle Nigel said the will o' the wisps only venture out at night," he said. "They must have a lair they return to during the day. If they led Uncle Nigel anywhere, it was probably back to that lair." He turned to the peat cutters. "You men must have some idea of where the will o' the wisps rise from, surely?"

They gave a collective shrug. All except for the man with the mismatched eyebrows, who nodded knowingly.

"They come from Hell," he intoned. "They are Satan's creatures. It is best, when seeing one, to say a prayer and swiftly turn the other way. Except for your uncle, no man was ever foolish enough to—" He paused abruptly, as if suddenly changing what he'd been about to say. "Nobody has ever wanted to tempt God's hand by getting so close to them."

Most of the peat cutters sadly shook their heads. The redhead, however, shrugged. "But Mister Owen paid well. The equivalent of a month's wages, just to tug on some ropes."

Several peat cutters nodded.

"What, exactly, are you implying?" Kenneth asked the man with the mismatched eyebrows. He knew of course. Full well. The peat cutters thought Uncle Nigel was foolish to have gone after a will o' the wisp. But he was a creature catcher. A professional. Kenneth balled his fists.

Old Tom touched Kenneth's arm. "Now, now, Herr Kenneth. No need for anger. These men are trying to help."

A peat cutter with a craggy face spread his callused hands. "We tried to warn your uncle about going after the willies, young Master Owen, but he insisted—"

"What did you just call them?" Kenneth asked.

The man frowned. "Willies. That's what my Gran always called them."

Kenneth slapped a hand against his forehead. "That's it!" he cried. "Willies!"

Candace gave him a quizzical look. "What about them?"

"The pixies," Kenneth told her. "They said they were going to dance me there."

Candace's look of puzzlement deepened. "I think they danced you around in a circle one too many times. You're not making any sense."

Kenneth gave an exasperated sigh. "One of the pixies said," he repeated slowly, "that they should 'dance me to the willies.' Then another pixie said the willies 'already had one.' They must have been talking about the will o' the wisps that lured Uncle Nigel away. They might know where he is!"

Old Tom inclined his head in a slight bow. "Clever thinking, Herr Owen."

The peat cutters murmured to each other. Several nodded excitedly.

Candace stared enviously at him. There was no getting around it: Kenneth had been the one to come up with the solution to the problem of finding Uncle Nigel. He allowed himself a small smirk.

"Yes, that was clever thinking, Kenneth," Candace

grudgingly admitted. "But what's wanted now is diplomacy. We need to talk the pixies into leading us to the spot." She turned to the men. "Have any of you a handkerchief?"

The peat cutters shook their heads.

"A handkerchief?" Kenneth sputtered. "What for? So we can wave a white flag and hope the pixies don't stab us?"

Candace rolled her eyes. "No, silly. A handkerchief is a traditional pixie offering of goodwill. Everyone knows that."

Kenneth shook his head. What a silly notion. It must have been another from the *Girl's Own Annuals*. "It's rocks that are wanted, not flags," he told his sister. "Big rocks. Bowl a few of the pixies over, and the rest will talk."

"No, they won't," Candace said. "They'll just run away and hide."

"Not if we capture one. We'll make him lead us to Uncle Nigel."

"Wrong," Candace said. "We've got to *persuade* the pixies to tell us where Uncle Nigel is. Otherwise they'll just lead us around in circles and have us dancing again."

Kenneth folded his arms across his chest. "And how are we supposed to persuade them?" he said in a scornful voice. "By appealing to their better natures—which they don't have—or by saying 'pretty please'?"

The peat cutters had been glancing back and forth between the two children all this while, like spectators at a tennis match. Now they waited for Candace's reply. She stood, fuming, obviously at a loss for a words.

It was Rumblegut who spoke first. "'Tis tae late for either gabbin' or brayin'," the troll said. "If yon pixies ken where thine uncle lies, they'll be on their way there now, since they nae longer hold either of ye two bairns captive."

Candace's angry expression instantly melted. Worry flashed across her face. "And . . . when the pixies get there?"

"They'll eat him."

Kenneth swallowed down the lump in his throat. They no longer had until sunset to find Uncle Nigel. For all they knew, the pixies might have reached him already. Even now, they might be carving his body into pixie-sized roasts with Kenneth's own pocketknife.

Candace's heart sank. Surely the pixies wouldn't *eat* Uncle Nigel. Surely not that.

Old Tom looked as grim as Candace felt. He turned to the peat cutters. "We shall search again. You men will return to the bog. Some shall go left, and some shall go right. We must find Herr Owen before the pixies do."

The peat cutters nodded. Old Tom drew them aside and began dividing them into two groups.

"Right," Kenneth said. He pointed toward the east. "The ruin lies in that direction, and the bog lies—" He used his other hand to point to where the peat cutters had come from. "There." He sighted alternately along one finger, then the next. "If the ruin is there . . . and the bog is there . . . and if the pixies make straight from one to the other, we should be able to pick up their trail somewhere along a line between the two."

"There won't be any trail," Candace protested. "Pixie dust only shows up in the moonlight."

"They'll leave footprints."

"Tiny ones that will be hard to spot," Candace said. "And the Moorlands will be covered with prints; Uncle Nigel said the pixies were everywhere. Besides, once the footprints reach the bog, they'll end. The pixies will wade into it, just as Uncle Nigel did. How will we follow them across water?"

Kenneth's face reddened. He dropped his arms. "Ah. Yes. Well."

Candace didn't have time to savor this small victory, however. Quick as a flash, Kenneth's eyes brightened. "The pixies are tiny," he countered. "Barely ankle-high. The water will be over their heads. They won't wade. They'll swim."

"What of it?" Candace asked. "Wade or swim, we'll lose their trail either way."

That silenced Kenneth. But only for a moment. "The ones at the ruin hadn't swum anywhere."

"How would you know?"

Kenneth looked smug. "They knew the will o' the wisps had Uncle Nigel, so they must have been on the lake already. But their clothes weren't wet."

"So?"

"So they must have used boats." Kenneth turned to Rumblegut. "Right, troll? We just have to look for their boats."

"Nae, lad. Pixies dinnae have boats."

Candace felt exasperated. It was as though she and Kenneth were going round in circles, like water down a drain. She turned to Rumblegut. "If the pixies don't use boats and they don't swim, then how will they get across the bog, to wherever Uncle Nigel is?"

"With the aid of the nixies, like as nowt."

"What are nixies?" Kenneth asked.

"Water spirits."

Candace nodded. She'd seen a drawing of nixies in a book of faerie stories by the Brothers Gentle. The spirits were able to assume vaguely human form, although their skin and hair were translucent as water. They made their beds on blood-red water lilies that drifted about on lakes.

Except, she supposed, that this would all be wrong. Just like the *Girl's Own Annual* had been wrong about pixies. She glanced up at Rumblegut. "I suppose you're going to tell me that nixies drink blood, or something equally unpleasant."

The troll's eyebrows rose. "How did thee know that, lass?"

Candace sighed. "A lucky guess."

"'Tis how thee can persuade nixies tae perform a service for ye," Rumblegut added. "By letting 'em drink three drops of thy blood. Yon pixies, like as nowt, fed 'em blood for the use of their lily pads."

"As boats?" Kenneth asked.

Rumblegut grinned. "Nae. As rafts. Yon nixies will tow them from below."

Kenneth made a sour face.

Candace was too busy thinking to enjoy the fact that

the troll was teasing Kenneth. The Brothers Gentle had at least got the lily pad part of the story right. "So all we have to do is look for lily pads moving about on the surface of the bog."

"Aye," Rumblegut said. "With pixies on 'em."

"I know!" Kenneth said. "We'll use the dirigible. We'll be able to spot the lily pads easily from the air, as long as we don't go too high up."

Old Tom returned to where the children stood, a worried look on his face. "And who will fly the dirigible?" he asked. He glanced up at the enormous gas bag. "Herr Owen and I have discussed ballast, and moorage, but I have not yet learned how to operate the craft."

"I can fly it," Kenneth said. "Uncle Nigel taught me."

Old Tom's eyebrows rose.

Candace opened her mouth to tell Old Tom that Kenneth's only "lesson" had been a ten-minute stint at the controls—then shut it again. Something more pressing than Kenneth's fib was troubling her. "When we do find the lily pads," she said slowly, "how are we to rescue Uncle Nigel?"

Kenneth shrugged. "Why, by jumping down into the water, I suppose."

Candace shook her head. "Didn't you hear what Rumblegut said? The will o' the wisps lure their victims out into *deep* water. And Uncle Nigel's a big man. If his bod—" She stopped, unable to say the word. "If he's in deep water, we may not be able to find him. Even by jumping in."

"We'll think of something once we get there," Kenneth said. He was bouncing on the balls of his feet like a boxer, something he did when he was excited. He turned toward the peat cutters. "You there—you men. Man the lines. We're taking off!"

Rumblegut turned to go. "Well, good luck tae ye, then, bairns. I hope thee finds thine uncle."

"Rumblegut, wait," Candace called after him. "We need your help."

The troll hesitated. "Aye? With what?"

"Somebody's going to need to wade into the water, once the pixies have been found," she said. "Somebody tall."

The troll looked around. "Oh, aye? And who would that be?"

"You," Candace said. "Even in the deepest part of the bog, your head will be above water. You're the only one who will be able to reach down and lift Uncle Nigel out."

The troll stared at her. "And why would I want tae do that?"

Candace hesitated. Wasn't it obvious? "Why—to save him, of course."

"But he's a *catcher*. To him, I'm nowt but a trophy. Why should he be anything tae me?"

"Because—" Candace was at a loss. Why indeed should Rumblegut care? Tears prickled the corners of her eyes. She tried to think about what to say next, but it was no use. She couldn't think of any argument that would sway the troll. "Because he's my uncle and I love him," she said at last. "And I thought—" She sniffled. "I thought that you were my friend."

Kenneth stepped forward. "She's right, tro— ah, Rumblegut. We need your help if we're going to save Uncle Nigel." He glanced at Candace. "We need to work . . . together." He said it slowly, as if it was a foreign word he'd just that moment learned.

Candace took Kenneth's hand.

The troll took a deep breath, then let it out in a slow, gusty sigh. "Reet," he said. "I'll help thee, bairns. Though I dinna ken why. I must be barmy."

Candace's heart leaped. Rumblegut would help! "Oh, thank you!" she cried, flinging her arms around his great stony middle.

"None o' that, lass," the troll said, gently prying her off. "Thee'll bruise thyself."

Kenneth sat in the wicker pilot's chair as the peat cutters removed just enough ballast for the dirigible to lift slightly. Most of the rocks remained on board; with only two people in the gondola and without all of Uncle Nigel's equipment, the dirigible had more lift.

Old Tom stood just behind Kenneth, worrying his cap with his fingers. "You are certain you know how to fly this machine, Herr Kenneth?" he shouted over the thrum of the engines.

"Of course," Kenneth called back, although in

truth, he was a little nervous. "Uncle Nigel let me fly it all the way here. I've had plenty of practice."

Old Tom nodded, but looked uneasy.

Kenneth's eye ranged over the controls. Everything was ready. He'd tied a small square block of peat to each steering pedal so that his feet could reach them. The peat was light enough that it didn't weigh the pedals down. His right hand rested on the wheel that was mounted on the side of the pilot's chair; his left hand was on the lever that controlled the engine speed.

Outside, the peat cutters held the lines, acting as human anchors to keep the dirigible from drifting. Candace and Rumblegut stood a short distance away, watching. Candace lifted a hand and waved. Kenneth gave her a grin and a thumbs up. At Old Tom's signal, one of the peat cutters scrambled up the mooring mast and cast off the dirigible's nose line. Old Tom motioned again, and the other men tugged on their lines, walking the dirigible clear of the mast.

"All is ready, Herr Kenneth."

Kenneth nodded, his stomach tight with anticipation. He waved to the peat cutters to let go of the lines. As they moved away, leaving the lines dangling, he eased the lever forward, at the same time spinning the wheel back slightly to bring the nose up. The dirigible moved forward, its nose rising. Kenneth barely managed to suppress a grin. He was doing it! The dirigible was taking off.

Then came a lurch that sent Old Tom staggering as the tail of the dirigible struck the ground. Outside, the peat cutters shouted. Kenneth saw several of them running away. The mooring mast loomed large in the port windows; Kenneth jammed his right foot down to turn the dirigible away. The dirigible, however, didn't respond. It just kept pivoting on its tail. Belatedly, Kenneth realized that this was because the tail was dragging along the ground—that was where the rudder was.

The dirigible crashed into the mast, bending it. Then, with a loud splintering sound, the top of the mast snapped off. As the dirigible lurched free, Kenneth was tossed to the side, jerking his hand away from the wheel. No longer held, the wheel spun crazily and the rear of the dirigible rose. Suddenly level again, the craft surged forward. But not in a straight line. The rudder was jammed, sending the dirigible around in a tight turn. Back toward the broken mast.

Heart pounding, Kenneth worked the pedals, trying to steer the dirigible away from the now jagged mooring mast. The rudder came unstuck, but suddenly there was nothing under his right foot. The block of peat that had been tied to the pedal had fallen off. Kenneth tried to compensate, but then the ties holding the other block of peat loosened and it fell off too.

As Kenneth scrambled to find the pedals again, the dirigible drew ever closer to the broken mooring mast. If it struck it, the gasbag might be torn open. Kenneth heard Old Tom shouting something and caught a glimpse of the troll running forward, but was too busy sliding down in his seat to reach the pedals to pay more attention than that.

At last his right foot found the pedal. Pushing hard on it, he tried to send the dirigible into a turn, but the craft responded sluggishly. It continued right over the spot where the broken mooring mast was. But there was no tearing sound, no sudden descent. The gasbag must have cleared the mooring mast. When he looked back, Kenneth saw the troll holding the broken mooring mast, which it had bent toward the ground like a bow. The peat cutters and Candace stared at the dirigible with open mouths, obviously amazed that it remained intact.

Hands shaking, Kenneth eased the wheel back a little. Slowly, this time. The nose of the dirigible gradually rose.

Old Tom picked himself up off the floor. With a visible effort, he composed himself. "Herr Kenneth," he said in a tight voice. "You told me . . . you knew . . . how to fly this machine."

"We're all right now," Kenneth reassured him, glancing out the window. The dirigible was just where he wanted it, at an altitude of about fifty feet. The ground slid briskly along below. Kenneth gave an experimental press on each of the pedals; they felt a little stiff, but the dirigible was capable of turning. The rudder hadn't broken, then. "Just a bit of a bumpy start, that's all. It's just that the controls are a bit more . . . sensitive than I'm used to."

Old Tom said nothing for several moments. Then he muttered something under his breath in German.

Kenneth wondered what he'd said. It didn't sound complimentary.

Old Tom pointed out the window. "The bog is that way. There—you see the sunlight glinting off the water?"

Kenneth nodded, glancing at the controls. The dirigible was moving along at a good clip. Working the pedals, Kenneth steered it to follow the twin lines the pony cart had pressed into the peat. After a few minutes the edge of the bog came into view and Kenneth spotted Uncle Nigel's equipment on the shore. A camera stood on a tripod beside the water. Near it was a wooden cabinet only slightly smaller than a steamer trunk, topped with a spiral of thick copper wire.

Kenneth felt a hollow sensation in his chest as the dirigible passed directly over the device. From the way Old Tom touched his own chest, Kenneth could tell he felt it too.

"It is as if—" Old Tom paused, searching for the word. "As if something were reaching inside me, trying to take something out."

"Not a very pleasant feeling," Kenneth observed.

"*Nein.*"

The dirigible moved out over the water. Kenneth turned left to follow the shoreline. His plan was to first search along the shore, at roughly the point where the pixies would have reached the water, assuming they headed for it in a straight line from the ruined cottage. If that didn't turn up any sign of them, he'd look elsewhere. Maybe closer to the center of the bog.

He eased the lever back until the dirigible was moving at no more than a man's walking pace, then held it at an altitude of about thirty feet above the bog, low enough for the ends of the lines trailing from the gas bag to brush against the water below, and peered out the window. Old Tom kept an equally vigilant watch out the other side of the gondola. The water below was black as coal and shiny as glass; Kenneth could see clouds reflected in it. Here and there he saw a clump of floating vegetation or a bubble rippling the surface, but no lily pads. At least, none with pixies on them.

"Nothing," Kenneth muttered. He brought the dirigible about, turning it in a wide arc. "Let's head for the middle of the bog. I'll bet he's there."

Old Tom frowned. "What makes you so certain?"

Kenneth shrugged. "Just a hunch."

"If I might suggest, Herr Kenneth, another course of action?"

Kenneth didn't like being told what to do. But he liked the sound of that. Action. "What?"

"We should cross the bog back and forth, like so," Old Tom said, moving his hand in a zigzag fashion. "Parallel to the shoreline, moving gradually out."

"That will take too much time," Kenneth protested.

"It would be more thorough. And that is what will find your uncle. A thorough search, not a haphazard one."

"But—"

"Herr Kenneth, we should not waste time arguing."

"I'm not arguing."

Old Tom paused. "Ah," he said a moment later. "I see. You are unable to steer the dirigible with such precision. That is why you protest."

Kenneth fumed. He'd show Old Tom. He turned the dirigible and made another pass along the shoreline—farther out, this time. When that was done, he made another turn and tried to repeat the process, but the dirigible kept turning this way and that, like a sailboat tacking in the wind. There were huge areas of the bog they were missing. Kenneth peered impatiently out the window. Still no lily pads.

After the fourth turn, he spotted Rumblegut. The troll was squatting by the water's edge a short distance from Uncle Nigel's equipment. The pony cart had pulled to a halt beside the troll; Candace sat on it, holding the reins. The peat cutters had followed and were standing in a cluster. Each of them had his head tipped back, watching the dirigible. Kenneth waved, but they were probably too far away to see him.

Once Kenneth located the pixies and tossed out the marker, the plan was for Rumblegut to wade out into the water, toward the spot over which the dirigible hovered. For now, however, all the troll and Candace could do was wait.

Kenneth was much happier *doing* something. Even if it wasn't producing any results.

He returned his attention to the water below. Every now and then he sneaked a glance at Old Tom.

"Is it true?" Kenneth asked at last. "Are you really a lycanthrope?"

Old Tom gave Kenneth a wary look. Slowly, he nodded his head.

"And Uncle Nigel doesn't know it?"

"He does not. And—" Old Tom hesitated. "I would prefer that he does not learn of it."

"Why not?"

"He might . . . dismiss me, if he knew."

"Dismiss you?" Kenneth said. "Nonsense. Why, you've been in his employ for twelve years. Uncle Nigel knows the value of loyalty; he wouldn't dismiss a servant just because that man turns into a wolf once a month."

Old Tom returned his attention to the window. "But I am not a man."

"Of course you are," Kenneth said. "Well, aside from last night, that is. But that hardly counts."

"It counts," Old Tom said. "When I am . . . in the grip of the moon, I have little control over my impulses. And I am . . . infectious. If your uncle saw me then, he would confine me to an asylum."

"But Uncle Nigel *likes* you."

Old Tom stared out the window. Several seconds passed. "Herr Kenneth, we should be concentrating on the search. If you would please return your attention to the water below."

Kenneth did, but his mind was elsewhere. Perhaps, when they got back, he'd tell the other boys at his school that he'd been infected with lycanthropy. That cut on his ankle the pixies gave him with the pocketknife—he could pass that off as a werewolf bite. A graze. When the boys teased him for being smaller, he could growl at them and tear open the collar of his shirt, and warn them all that he'd *get* them, sure, once the next full moon came along.

Unless Old Tom was right about werewolves winding up in asylums. If Kenneth's act was too convincing, they might just lock him up in an asylum too. He remembered the screams he'd heard echoing from behind the barred windows of Bedlam Asylum, and shuddered.

It was time to bring the dirigible around again. Sliding down in the pilot's chair, Kenneth worked the rudder pedals. The dirigible turned. They were near the middle of the bog now, and Kenneth was starting to wonder if they'd ever see anything. He glanced out the window—then stared down intently as he saw a dozen circular objects floating on the surface of the water, off to the left. Tiny figures were moving around on top of them: the pixies.

"There!" Kenneth cried. "I see them!"

Old Tom hurried to his side of the gondola. "*Ja!* I see them also. Fly closer."

As the dirigible droned closer to the spot where the lily pads were, the pixies looked up. Kenneth could see, now that they were halted, the lily pads forming a circle around a wide patch of water. Sunlight glinted off an object lying on one of the lily pads: the blade of Kenneth's pocketknife. As the dirigible approached, the pixies stared upward.

Kenneth cut the engines, but the dirigible kept going. It soared over the pixies, leaving them behind.

"Blast!" Kenneth shouted. Belatedly, he realized he should have cut the engines earlier, when he first spotted the pixies. Slamming open the engine-speed lever, he brought the dirigible around in as tight a turn as it could manage. Slowly, the dirigible turned.

"Ready the marker, Tom," Kenneth shouted.

Old Tom ran to the gondola door and lifted a large ballast rock. A rope was tied to it; at the other end of the rope was an empty barrel that had held drinking water. The barrel was topped with a pole that bore a makeshift flag of white cloth, something Rumblegut would be able to see at a distance. As the dirigible passed over the pixies again, Old Tom threw open the door. Legs braced, the rock cradled in his arms, he waited for Kenneth's command.

"Now!" Kenneth shouted as the lily pads slid by below.

Old Tom hurled the rock, then leaped out of the way as the rope dragged the barrel out after it. Kenneth's stomach lurched as the dirigible rose sharply.

He pressed his face to the window, watching to see where the rock fell. It landed with a splash just beyond the lily pads. The ripples of its splash rocked them a moment later. Then the barrel hit, sending out another set of ripples. The pixies fell to their knees, clinging to their bobbing lily pads.

Kenneth saw with relief that they'd guessed right on the necessary length of rope. Had it been too short, the rock might have pulled the barrel underwater. The barrel, however, was floating on the surface, its flag upright.

"We did it!" he shouted.

Now it was up to Candace and Rumblegut.

As Old Tom shut the door, Kenneth brought the dirigible around again. This time, he killed the engines long before they reached the spot where the barrel bobbed. Slowly, silently, they drifted toward the lily pads, gradually coming to a stop. Kenneth whooped as he saw that he'd timed it perfectly: the dirigible had halted just beyond the lily pads. From here, he could throw stones at the pixies, keep them busy ducking while Rumblegut waded out to this spot.

Old Tom, however, didn't seem to share Kenneth's joy. He stared down at the water, a worried expression on his face.

"Herr Kenneth," he said. "There is a problem. The pixies grabbed hold of the lines as we passed over them the second time. They are climbing."

Kenneth opened the window next to him, peered out, and swore softly under his breath. Then he grabbed the wheel. If it was a fight the pixies wanted, he would give them one.

9

Candace and Rumblegut reached the edge of the bog just as the dirigible began its turn. It cruised parallel with the shore, making long sweeps over the bog. Candace watched as it slowly came about, the distant sound of its engines droning across the water.

The peat cutters stood near the pony cart, watching the dirigible and talking in low voices. Candace had persuaded them to come this far, despite their fear of will o' the wisps. They'd promised to stay, but only until sunset. Then they'd leave, whether Uncle Nigel had been found or not.

Hopefully Kenneth would locate the pixies before then. At sunset, the will o' the wisps would come out, and they'd all be in danger.

Candace climbed out of the pony cart and limped over to where Uncle Nigel's equipment stood. A camera stood on its tripod, close to the water's edge. A little farther along the shore was a large rectangular cabinet that stood as high as Candace was tall, connected by wires to half a dozen ceramic battery boxes, each twice the size of a loaf of bread.

A loud humming noise came from inside the cabinet. Mounted on the top of it was a squared-off spiral of stout copper wire with the approximate shape of an upside-down pyramid. Even in daylight, Candace could see sparks dancing along the wire. The device seemed to draw these sparks out of the air itself; every few seconds a tiny fork of lightning appeared in the air just above the wire, then struck it. Each time this happened, Candace's skin tingled and the hairs on her arms stood erect, as if she'd just shivered.

Rumblegut ambled closer and sniffed. "Smells as like the air itself be afire," he remarked. He peered at the device. "'Tis the machine thine uncle hoped would catch will o' the wisps?"

Candace nodded.

"How does it work?"

"I've no idea, aside from the fact that it's an 'electrical net.' That's what Uncle Nigel called it."

The troll peered into the sky, as if expecting to see a net suspended in midair. Then Candace realized he was watching a dragonfly buzzing lazily above the cabinet.

The peat cutters—particularly the man with mismatched eyebrows—seemed to be disturbed by the device. Candace could hear him muttering that it might draw will o' the wisps out of the bog, even in daytime. More of that, and the men would leave sooner, rather than later. In a pinch, Candace supposed, Rumblegut could hold the dirigible steady all by himself. But the peat cutters might be required for other tasks. To fetch a local doctor, should Uncle Nigel need medical assistance, for example.

The peat cutters eventually fell silent—all but the nearsighted redhead, who was loudly asking the others what was going on and when they could expect to collect the balance of their pay.

If Candace could turn the creature-catching device off, perhaps the peat cutters might feel less anxious. She studied the cabinet. It had a half-dozen glass-fronted gauges, each with a needle that held steady on a numbered line. She had no idea what they signified. She saw no obvious on-off switch, but there was a crank on one side, its handle covered in a thick sleeve of rubber. She cautiously touched it with a finger, half expecting to get a shock. Then she grasped the crank firmly. Taking a deep breath, she turned it clockwise for several revolutions, as far as it would go.

The humming noise immediately got louder and the needles in the gauges began to move. The tiny lightning bolts—which had been materializing and striking the wire at about one every three or four seconds—now flashed into existence at a rate nearly as swift as the pounding of Candace's heart. *Crack-crack, crack-crack, crack-crack!* Candace's skin tingled, and her hair lifted off her shoulders.

"Lass," Rumblegut said, "I've a bad feeling—"

"Sorry," Candace shouted over the static. "I've turned it the wrong way. I'll have it off soon enough."

She spun the crank in the opposite direction. The lightning bolts and sparks slowed, and the humming became quieter. So far, so good, but the device didn't shut down. Instead it sped up again. Now the sparks moved *up* the wire, sending lightning bolts crackling out of its tip. The more Candace turned the crank, the larger these forks of lightning became.

Candace could hear the alarmed babble of the peat cutters. Rather than turn the crank any further, she rotated it back to where it had been when she started. The sparks resumed their slow progression down the wire. She considered unhooking the batteries from the device—that would stop it, she was certain—but was afraid the disconnected wires might give her a shock. She decided, in the end, to just leave the cabinet alone.

Rumblegut stooped and gently prodded something on the ground with a massive finger. Glancing down, Candace saw it was the dragonfly. The bright blue insect lay on its back, wings twitching. She wondered if a fork of lightning from her uncle's device had struck it.

Footsteps squelched across the wet peat. The man with mismatched eyebrows. He halted well back from the circle of batteries and wires. "You shouldn't be playing with that cabinet, Miss. It's the Devil's own work."

"No, it's not," Candace said defiantly. "It's my uncle's."

The man's lips tightened. "Exactly."

Candace took a deep breath, reminding herself to remain calm. She silently repeated the old adage that Nurse frequently used: honey catches more flies than vinegar. This fellow was as annoying as the mosquitoes buzzing around her face, but she might need him. He was afraid, she reminded herself. Afraid of the unknown. She just had to calm him down. She would not—would *not*—reply in kind to his rude remarks. She'd seen, on more than one occasion, her mother do that and lose any allies she might have had.

She folded her hands together and spoke in a soothing voice. "Mister—?"

"Bitteridge," he said, supplying his name.

"Mister Bitteridge," she continued, "my uncle's device is a defense against will o' the wisps, and therefore a weapon against Satan. I should think it would have your blessing."

Bitteridge looked uncertain. "Yes, well—"

Rumblegut stood. "Who's Satan?" he asked in a low voice. "Another catcher?"

"He is that," Bitteridge said earnestly. "A catcher of souls. But, being a soulless creature who knows neither right nor wrong, you would have no knowledge of him."

Rumblegut's eyes bulged. "Soulless?" He glared. "'Tis all living things what has souls." He jerked a thumb at the nest on his shoulder. "Why, just look at yon spuggies, and how the ma coddles her cletch. She loves 'em, much as humans care for they own bairns."

"Humans have souls," Bitteridge said, folding his arms across his chest. "Animals and brutish beasts, on the other hand, do n—"

"Brutish beast, am I?" the troll rumbled. "Why, thee scaumy little—"

Candace touched the troll's arm. "Rumblegut," she hissed. "Ignore the insult. Please."

Rumblegut shook off her hand and stomped toward Bitteridge, setting the ground quivering. The troll loomed over him, teeth bared. The peat cutter closed his eyes and whispered a quick prayer.

"Miss," he said in a tight voice, "please call off your troll."

Rumblegut glanced at Candace and gave her a sly wink. "What do ye say, miss?" he rumbled. He raised a fist. "Should I thump him?"

Candace had to work at hiding her smile. She tilted her head, as if seriously considering Rumblegut's offer. "I think not," she said at last. "I'm sure Mr. Bitteridge will apologize." She paused. "Won't you, Mr. Bitteridge?"

"To a troll?" Bitteridge sputtered.

Rumblegut clamped a hand on Bitteridge's shoulder. The peat cutter shrank back. His Adam's apple bobbed up and down as he swallowed. Hard. At last he nodded. "My apologies, Rumplebelly."

"Rumblegut."

Bitteridge gave a nervous laugh. "Rumblegut."

The troll loomed closer, pressing down on Bitteridge's shoulder. "*Mister* Rumblegut."

Bitteridge opened his mouth. Closed it. Opened it again. He looked like a gasping fish. Except that he was trying to get something out, not in. "Mister Rumblegut."

Rumblegut grinned and released him.

Bitteridge ran the back of his sleeve across his brow, wiping away sweat. He glanced back at the other peat cutters, who were watching the exchange with wide eyes, then returned his attention to Candace. "The point remains," he said in a slightly steadier voice, "that you shouldn't meddle with that device, Miss Owen. It's not something you'd be capable of understanding."

"But I only meant to shut it off," Candace protested.

Bitteridge nodded. "All well and good. But that's best left to Old Tom. Or to Master Kenneth."

Candace's eyes narrowed. "Why is that?"

"You're a girl."

Candace felt her cheeks flush an angry red. "And—?"

"And girls don't have a mind for mechanical things."

Candace's eyes narrowed. "At least I'm not afraid to touch it," she retorted. "You, on the other hand—" Then she realized what she was doing: calling the man a coward. "Oh!" she blurted out. "I didn't mean to imply . . . That is . . . "

Bitteridge drew himself up in a huff. "Tell your uncle," he said in a flinty voice, "that he can keep the balance of my pay. I'll not be continuing in his employ any longer."

That said, he turned on his heel and strode back to where the other peat cutters stood. A babble of conversation followed, and then Bitteridge took the pony's reins in hand. Without so much as a glance back, he led it away. The cart trundled behind, its wheels gently creaking.

The other peat cutters stood for several moments, glancing back and forth between Candace and the departing cart, then picked up their tools and followed Bitteridge.

"Please!" Candace said. "Don't go."

A couple of the peat cutters gave her apologetic looks and touched their caps, but they continued to trudge away. All but one: the red-headed fellow with the squinting eyes. He walked toward where Candace stood, stumbled over a wire, caught his footing again, and then halted, peering uncertainly about. Taking off his cap, he nodded in Candace's general direction.

"Don't worry, Miss. I'm staying. I'll man the lines for you."

Candace sighed. She doubted the red-headed man could find his own bootstraps, let alone a line trailing through the air. Even so, she wasn't going to make the same mistake twice. "Thank you, Mister—"

"Cumberstone."

"Mister Cumberstone. I'm sure you'll be of great assistance."

Cumberstone smiled.

Rumblegut leaned closer to Candace. "Don't ye fret none, lass. Ye dinnae need yon bickerish fellows."

"I suppose you're right," Candace said as she watched them go.

She turned just in time to see a barrel tumble out of the dirigible and land with a splash in the bog. "Kenneth's found the pixies!" she cried. "Let's go." She held up her arms for Rumblegut to pick her up, but the troll was staring out over the water.

"Summat's nae right," he said in an ominous voice.

He was right. The dirigible had silently coasted to a halt, but now its engines sprang back to life. Droning loudly, it dipped toward the bog in a rapid descent. Candace gasped as the bottom of the gondola struck the water with an audible splash. The dirigible came to a shuddering halt, its balloon bulging forward, then settling back again. Engines droning, the dirigible struggled to free itself from the water. Then, with a gurgle, the engines cut out. A moment later, the gasbag started to slump.

"The dirigible's crashed!" Candace cried.

Cumberstone squinted in the general direction of the bog. "It has?"

Candace tugged on Rumblegut's arm. "Hurry," she urged. "Kenneth needs our help."

"Aye," the troll said, scooping her into his arms. He strode out into the water, heading at a brisk clip for the spot where the dirigible had gone down, his strides cutting a frothing wake across the bog.

Cumberstone, standing alone on the shore, squinted this way and that. "Does this mean I won't get my pay?" He took a hesitant step. "Miss Owen? Where have you gone?" He took another step—only to trip on a wire and stumble into the cabinet, sending it rocking back and forth. Candace, glancing back over Rumblegut's shoulder, saw Cumberstone grab the device with both hands, either in an effort to steady himself or to prevent it from falling over. Then, abruptly, he let go. He twisted around and sat down, his back against the cabinet.

Which was just fine with Candace. The less Cumberstone moved about, the less damage he'd do. She turned back toward the dirigible, staring at it anxiously as Rumblegut splashed through the bog at a run.

As the pixies climbed the lines, Kenneth threw the switch that engaged the engines, then spun the wheel forward. The dirigible responded sluggishly, but eventually the nose dipped.

"Herr Kenneth!" Old Tom shouted. "We are falling!"

"I know," Kenneth shouted back, holding the wheel forward. "When those lines hit the water, the pixies will be torn off."

A tiny hand appeared on the sill of the window next to the captain's chair. A tiny green hand. A pixie hauled

itself upright on the sill. Suddenly noticing it, Kenneth tried to crank the window shut with his left hand while holding the wheel with his right. He wasn't quick enough. Before he could close the window, the pixie was inside. It held an acorn in one hand, ready for a throw. It hurled the nut right on target: into Kenneth's left eye.

"Ow!" Kenneth cried, squinting both eyes shut. He slammed his left fist blindly down on the window sill, on the spot where the pixie had been, but missed his target. Then he felt a fierce, hot pain in his thumb: the pixie, biting him. He tried to shake it off, but it clung to his hand like a ferret.

"Ow, ow, ow!" Kenneth shouted. His left eye stung fiercely. So did his hand. Both eyes were filled with tears; he could barely see.

"Herr Kenneth!" Old Tom shouted. "Release the wheel! The water—"

The gondola smacked into the bog with a loud splash. Kenneth was thrown against the front window, cracking it. Old Tom grabbed for the handle of the door, but was also thrown forward. The door's latch released, and the door flopped open. Bog water surged inside. The floor of the gondola leveled out as it was weighed down with water.

Kenneth slammed his left hand into the window frame, at last dislodging the pixie. It fell, squealing, into the water at his feet. Kenneth sloshed toward the door, Old Tom close on his heels. Together, they reached out and drew the door closed. By the time it was latched, the floor of the gondola was ankle-deep in water. And the pixie was inside Kenneth's trouser leg.

"Getitoutgetitout!" Kenneth cried, hopping on one foot and wrenching up his pants leg. The pixie was revealed, its teeth firmly sunk into Kenneth's calf.

"*Stillgestanden!*" Old Tom cried, obviously yelling at Kenneth to hold still. He dropped to all fours like a dog and grabbed the pixie with his teeth. Then he loped across the gondola and spat the pixie out the open window. He started to crank the window shut. Halfway through, he glanced up at the gasbag. "*Verdammt!*"

Kenneth had no idea what the word meant, but it sounded like Old Tom was upset about something. He sloshed across the dirigible and craned his neck to see what Old Tom was looking at. It was the pixie with the knife. It gave them a nasty grin, then plunged the knife into the bag. A gleeful look on its face, the pixie let go of the line it had climbed and clung to the handle of the knife, dragging it downward through the fabric. The blade opened a long, vertical gash in the gasbag, then slipped out. Knife and pixie tumbled into the water below. Bobbing about on the surface, the pixie looked up at the fluttering hole and laughed.

Kenneth cranked a window open to survey the damage. A steady hissing noise came from above. He sniffed. Couldn't smell gas. Nor could he see it. But it was there. Hydrogen. And the dirigible's motors were thrumming.

Kenneth scrambled toward the pilot's chair.

Old Tom looked startled. "Herr Kenneth, what is—"

Kenneth slammed home the switch, killing the engines. He let out a long, shaky sigh. Murky water sloshed about his ankles, stinging the cut the pixies had inflicted earlier with the knife. The gondola bobbed sluggishly as water continued to seep in through the closed door. The pixies had abandoned the ropes now, and were capering about on the ledges outside the windows.

One of them found the window Old Tom hadn't quite closed, and shouted to the others. She jumped inside and swam toward Old Tom, an evil glint in her eye. Old Tom crouched, mouth open, ready to bite, but the pixie was caught by a current. It carried her against one of the many cabinet doors that lined both walls of the gondola, and sucked her in through one of the slats.

Old Tom let out a bark of laughter, but Kenneth's eyes widened. That cabinet—the one the pixie had just been drawn into. It was the one Kenneth and Candace had stowed away inside, the one that held the batteries that powered the dirigible. As soon as the water climbed high enough, it would submerge the batteries. Short them out. When that happened, there would be sparks.

The ruptured gasbag continued to hiss. For now, the hydrogen was leaking upward. But when the gasbag settled onto the gondola, the hydrogen inside it would be closer to those batteries.

"Tom!" Kenneth shouted. "Get out! Get away from the dirigible!"

Old Tom half-rose from his crouch. "The pixies are no threat, Herr Kenneth. I can—"

"Get out!" Kenneth shrieked. He tried to push open the door, but the water was keeping it shut. "The dirigible is about to explode!"

Eyes suddenly wide, Old Tom reared to his feet and slammed his shoulder into the door.

Rumblegut and Candace were halfway to the dirigible when it exploded in an enormous orange fireball. Candace was so shocked, she didn't even cry out. She simply stared, struck mute. Finally, a word creaked out of her mouth. "Kenneth." Every inch of her body felt cold. She found herself breathing rapidly. Shivering.

The troll halted and cursed under his breath, a low sound like rock cracking. He stared at the burning dirigible for several seconds. Then he burst into a run.

Water splashed in great sheets with each step. Candace was jostled up and down, despite being clasped firmly against Rumblegut's chest. His rough skin scraped against her; his tight grip drove the air from her lungs each time she bounced about. Filthy water splashed into her face, plastering her hair against her scalp and turning her clothes sodden. She didn't care. Her eyes were held by the dirigible, its ruptured balloon slumped over the lump that had been the gondola, sizzling as it burned, billowing a cloud of smoke and steam into the air.

She found herself whispering a prayer and silently promising to never, ever again, poke Kenneth in church and make him yelp in the middle of the sermon. "Please, God," she whispered. "Please save Kenneth. And poor Old Tom."

The closer the troll got to the burning dirigible, the deeper the water became. By the time they drew close to it, the water was up to Rumblegut's chest.

"Hold tight," he told her, heaving her up onto his shoulder. He cupped a hand around the bird's nest on his other shoulder, protecting it from splashes.

Candace, holding tight to Rumblegut's rough neck, looked around frantically. She could feel the heat of the burning gondola on her skin. The tattered gasbag was sopping up water and slowly smothering the fire. Steam hung thick in the air.

"*Fraulein!*" a voice called. "Over here!"

"Old Tom!" Candace could see him now, clinging to the barrel that bobbed in the water beyond where the dirigible had fallen. His gray hair and muttonchop sideburns were singed, and his face was red. He flashed Candace a quick smile, then winced.

Rumblegut waded toward him.

"Where's Kenneth?" Candace asked, looking wildly around. "Is he—"

"Below. Yes." Old Tom nodded down at the water. Strangely, he was smiling.

"Oh," Candace said. A small, sad sound.

Something burst out of the water from below, up through the lily pads. A boy's face, seen in profile. It was sputtering and blinking.

"Can't find him," the boy announced. Then he broke into a fit of coughing.

"Kenneth!" Candace cried.

Kenneth, treading water, spun in place. "About time you got here," he said. Then he grinned—and winced, just as Old Tom had. Kenneth's face was just as red. His eyebrows and hair looked funny. Burned off. "If you'd been a few minutes earlier, you might have got caught in the blast." Then he laughed. A little hysterically, Candace thought.

"I thought you were dead," Candace cried.

"Not me." Another laugh. A little less brittle, this time. "But some of the pixies might be."

Candace's breath caught. "Kenneth! You didn't . . . blow up the dirigible on purpose. Did you?"

Kenneth snorted. "What a stupid thing to say."

Oddly, Candace wasn't insulted. Instead, she felt relieved. Her brother hadn't gone crazy, then. No more than usual, at least.

Kenneth swam over to the barrel and caught hold of it, next to Old Tom. "That's better," he said, breathing heavily. "Now that Rumblegut's here, *he* can search."

"Yes," Candace said, remembering the reason they were here. She turned her attention to Rumblegut, who was watching the smoking gondola with a strange expression. It almost looked as though he were pleased about something. She had to knock on his head to get his attention. "Rumblegut, could you set me down in the water, please, and start looking for Uncle Nigel?"

"Aye," Rumblegut said. "I could." He jerked a thumb at his right shoulder. "But what of yon spuggies?"

Candace shook her head, wondering if she'd heard correctly. "What have the sparrows to do with it?"

Rumblegut nodded at the water that lapped at his chest. "'Tis deep. I'll have tae duck under for me hands tae touch bottom. Yon nest will be drowned, and me spuggies with it."

"Oh, is that all?" Kenneth asked peevishly.

The troll scowled at him and pointed a finger. "Ye'll nae speak that way about me spuggies, lad, if thee wants thine uncle found."

"I'm sure Kenneth didn't mean he wanted your poor dear sparrows to drown," Candace reassured him, giving her brother a vile look. "Did you, Kenneth?"

For once, Kenneth was quick to catch on. "'Course not," he said. He raised a dripping hand and jerked his thumb over his shoulder. "The water's quite shallow, just a short distance behind us. We can stand there while you feel about, Rumblegut. Candace can hold your nest."

Old Tom nodded vigorously. "*Ja*," he said. "The water is quite shallow, thank Gott. That allowed Kenneth and I to flee some distance before the dirigible exploded. I only wish," he added, his mouth turning down, "that we had not turned our heads to look at it." He touched his reddened face gingerly with a finger.

"Come on," Kenneth said, waving an arm. "Follow me."

He swam a short distance, then stood up in water that was only waist deep. Old Tom swam in the same direction, and likewise stood when he reached the shallow spot. Rumblegut followed, carefully skirting around the deep patch.

"Mind where you step!" Candace cautioned. "Uncle Nigel is under there somewhere."

Rumblegut nodded.

Reaching the spot where Kenneth and Old Tom stood, he lifted Candace down from his shoulder. She shivered as the water lapped around her waist. The blisters on her feet stung.

Rumblegut pointed at the nest. "Be careful," he rumbled. "Dinnae tip yon nest or me spuggies may tumble out."

Candace delicately pried the nest loose from the troll's shoulder. The fledglings inside it cheeped frantically at first, but a few soothing words soon quieted them. She knew better than to stroke them; the mother sparrow would abandon any fledglings that smelled of human.

Satisfied, Rumblegut waded back into the deep water. He took a deep breath and ducked under. Several minutes went by. Candace and Kenneth exchanged worried looks. Old Tom gave a nervous growl. Even the fledglings peeked over their nest and cheeped. A few bubbles broke on the surface of the bog where Rumblegut had gone down. Then the bubbles stopped.

Candace chewed her lip. "Do you think he's—"

Rumblegut's head and shoulders broke the water, sending ripples cascading outward. He gasped, then shook his head. "I cannae find any trace of him."

"Impossible," Kenneth said. "He must be there. Try again."

The troll shook his head. "Nae lad. He's nae here. There's nowt but mud." He raised a hand that was filled with soggy peat. "And—" He flattened his hand, palm up, and probed the handful of mud with his index finger, then pulled something from it: a knife. "This."

"My pocketknife!" Kenneth said.

Rumblegut handed it to him. Kenneth swished it about in the water that lapped at his waist, washing the mud from it, then carefully folded it shut.

Candace felt a rising sense of alarm. The sun would be setting soon. They had to find Uncle Nigel, and quickly. She could see faint glimmers within the water—were those will o' the wisps, getting ready to rise, or just reflected sunlight?

She turned to Kenneth. "Are you sure this is the right spot?"

Kenneth nodded stoutly. "Absolutely." He pointed at the lily pads that bobbed around the spot where Rumblegut stood. "There's the pixie's rafts."

Candace stared at the lily pads. They were green—not red, as the Brothers Gentle stories had said.

"Perhaps the pixies were mistaken," Old Tom said. "Perhaps they came to the wrong spot."

Candace thought about what Rumblegut had told them earlier. "The pixies didn't come here on their own," she told the others. "The nixies towed their lily pads here. They must have been able to see where Uncle Nigel is. All we have to do is ask them."

Kenneth slammed a fist into the water, sending up a splash. "You there: you nixies! Tell us where Uncle Nigel is."

"That's not the way," Candace said. She handed the nest to Old Tom. Then she pointed to the knife her brother held. "Give me that."

Kenneth reluctantly handed his pocketknife to his sister. "Don't drop it," he said.

"I won't." Candace opened the knife and held its point against the tip of her index finger. She took a deep breath, then poked her skin. Blood beaded on the tip of her finger. She squeezed it and a drop of her blood fell into the bog. Another. A third.

Then, most perplexing of all, she broke into a poem.

"Lovely as a flower, beautiful to see, I call to you, O Lorelei, come winging hence to me."

They waited.

Nothing happened.

Kenneth looked at Candace. "What made you think that would work?"

"It's a poem for calling nixies."

Kenneth snorted. "You've obviously got it wrong."

Candace blinked furiously. She looked as though she was about to cry. "I didn't get it wrong," she protested. "I remember it quite distinctly. It *has* to work."

Something swooped past, startling her so badly she

nearly fell over. It was the mother sparrow, back again to feed her young. If the situation hadn't been so desperate, Kenneth might have laughed. "The poem seems good for one thing, at least," he said sourly. "Sending a sparrow 'winging hence to thee.'"

Candace stared at him, wide-eyed. "That's it!" she cried. "That's precisely what's wrong, Kenneth!"

"What do you mean?" Kenneth asked, not understanding. "That it *is* a rhyme for summoning sparrows?"

Candace gave a giddy laugh. "No. Nixies don't 'wing,' they swim."

She pricked her finger a second time, and repeated the poem. Except that this time, she ended it with, "come swimming hence to me."

All at once, the water next to Rumblegut began to churn. The troll glanced down in alarm at the whirlpool that was forming next to him, then hurriedly waded to the shallows. Water streaming from his craggy body, he watched in silence as a shape slowly rose from the whirlpool.

It was the head of a woman. A woman about half the size of a human, with skin the color of frosted glass, hair that looked like flowing rivulets of clear water, and eyes whose vivid blue irises turned like a slow-moving whirlpool.

She spoke in a voice as soft as the hiss of gentle waves on a sandy beach. "Who calls Lorelei?"

Kenneth gaped. His sister had done it. Summoned

a nixie. "So where did you get that poem from?" he whispered.

"In a book," Candace whispered back. "You should try reading one, sometime."

Kenneth slowly nodded. Perhaps he would. Perhaps their father hadn't been entirely wrong about the value of research, after all.

Old Tom suddenly clapped a hand across his eyes. Kenneth wondered why; the murky water hid the nixie from the chin down, preserving her modesty. He supposed she must be naked, and wondered if the rest of her would be as lovely as her face. He stared at her, dreamily imagining marrying a girl like that, one day. He'd been shivering, a little, from the water's chill. Now a warm glow suffused his body. The nixie's whirlpool eyes seemed to pull him closer. He took a step toward her . . .

Rumblegut's hand clapped heavily down upon Kenneth's shoulder, startling him. "I thought thee too young," the troll rumbled in a low voice. Then he chuckled. "Thee'd best cover thine eyes, as well. Human boys cannae resist nixie magic like trolls can."

Kenneth, suddenly aware that the nixie had been casting a spell on him, complied. He shuddered at the thought that he'd been about to wade out into deep water, just to be near her. He wondered if nixies did that to drown people, the way will o' the wisps did.

Candace, however, seemed unaffected by the nixie's magic. Kenneth heard her talking to the creature, asking it—oh, so sweetly—to show them where Uncle Nigel was. There was silence as the nixie considered the request. Then she spoke.

"Will thee give unto me thy promise of a boon, should I one day ask one of thee?" its fluid voice murmured.

"I will," Candace said.

"Seal thine oath with an offering," the nixie said. "A lock of thy hair."

Kenneth held his breath. Would Candace agree? He had a bad feeling about this. The nixie's request made him think of the locks of hair that were snipped from the heads of dead people and made into mourning jewelry. He wondered if the nixie was going to tie the hair into a knot and mount it on a brooch, as Mrs. Soames had done after her husband died.

"Here you are," Candace said.

Kenneth risked a peek between his fingers. Candace held a lock of hair in one hand, the open pocketknife in her other hand. The nixie plucked the blonde hair from Candace's fingers and disappeared, leaving only ripples behind. Candace slowly folded the pocketknife shut, a worried expression on her face.

Kenneth lowered his hands. "Did she—"

Before he could complete his question, the nixie reappeared. She beckoned with one hand, a hand that Kenneth imagined stroking his cheek . . .

Rumblegut nudged him. Kenneth closed his eyes. But not before he saw what the nixie had brought to the surface. She'd lifted a body from the bottom of the bog. Most of the body was underwater, obscured by the water's murkiness, but the nixie had raised one of its hands out of the water to show them. It was a man's hand, firmly clenched around the shaft of a distinctive silver-capped walking stick.

Uncle Nigel.

**10**

Candace formally thanked the nixie, giving as graceful a curtsey as she was able while standing in waist-deep water. Then she pulled Rumblegut forward. The troll waded back into the deep water and reached under the surface, taking Uncle Nigel from the nixie.

The nixie released Uncle Nigel and sank back into the bog, leaving only ripples behind.

Candace trembled. She'd been both praying for and dreading this moment. Uncle Nigel had been underwater a long time—since sometime last night. By all logic, he should be dead. Candace had never seen the victim of a drowning, but she had once seen an illustration, in the *Londinium Times*, of a boy who'd been pulled from the Thames. The drawing had shown him lying limp in the arms of his grieving mother, his eyes closed. Nurse had snatched away the newspaper after seeing what Candace was reading, but the image had stuck with her. Would Uncle Nigel look the same way, his face slack and drained of color, his eyes closed? Or would the will o' the wisps' magic have preserved him, as Rumblegut had said?

She reached for Kenneth's hand. He grasped hers, his own hand trembling. Old Tom placed an arm around each of the twins' shoulders and stood behind them, waiting.

Rumblegut gently lifted Uncle Nigel's body out of the bog. Water streamed from it. Uncle Nigel's thick dark hair was plastered against his scalp and his eyes were closed. His arms and legs hung limp, but oddly, his right hand continued to grip his walking stick.

Candace felt Kenneth give her hand a reassuring squeeze as Rumblegut waded back toward the shallow water where they stood.

"We've done it," he whispered. "Saved him."

Candace glanced into her brother's eyes. Despite his brave words, he looked as worried as she felt.

Rumblegut reached the shallows and squatted, cradling Uncle Nigel's body in his arms. Candace stared at her uncle's face. His thick black mustache hung limp over his upper lip and the scar on his left cheek was nearly invisible against the pallor of his skin. He didn't seem to be breathing. Rumblegut laid an ear against Uncle Nigel's chest and listened.

Candace swallowed back the lump that had risen in her throat. "Something's wrong, isn't it?"

"Is he dead?" Kenneth asked, his voice breaking.

"He should nae be," Rumblegut said. "Now that he's free of yon bog, he should be waking. The magic of yon will o' the wisps should hae kept thine uncle alive."

"But it didn't!" Candace quavered. "Did it?"

Kenneth stifled a sob. Candace started to cry.

"*Kinder*," Old Tom said, pulling them closer. "Be strong. Your uncle—"

"Is alive, but verra weak," Rumblegut said in a low voice. He shifted Uncle Nigel into the crook of his left arm and tapped a massive forefinger on Uncle Nigel's chest. *Thud-thud. Thud-thud. Thud-thud.* A rhythm like the slow beating of a heart.

"Herr Rumblegut, I fear Herr Owen is passing away."

Rumblegut glanced up at Candace, his blocky jaw clenched. He glanced at the western sky, where the sun was almost touching the horizon. "'Tis nae yet sunset," he said while tapping on Uncle Nigel's chest. *Thud-thud.* "'Till then," *thud-thud,* "'tis hope."

Candace's shoulders slumped. She opened her mouth, about to tell Rumblegut that it was over, that they were too late, to give up, when Kenneth suddenly cried out.

"Look!" he said, pointing.

Uncle Nigel's eyes were open. His chest rose and fell. He was alive!

Rumblegut gave a wide grin as Uncle Nigel coughed weakly. "Welcome back, catcher," he said softly.

But something was wrong. Uncle Nigel's chest rose and fell, but his eyes were unfocused. He made no move to look around, or to speak. He didn't even react to the fact that he was lying across the knees of a great troll that was peering down at him with a crystal-toothed grin. He just lay there.

Slowly, Rumblegut's grin faded. The troll waved a massive hand in front of Uncle Nigel's face. Nothing. No reaction. Except that Uncle Nigel at last let go of his walking stick. It splashed into the water. Kenneth grabbed it before it could float away.

Old Tom hurried forward and took Uncle Nigel's hand in his. "Herr Owen," he said. "Can you hear me? It is I, Thomas. Thomas Tiermann. You were drowned, Herr Owen, in the bog, but now you are rescued. Do you recognize me?" He leaned closer. "Can you see me?"

Uncle Nigel blinked. His eyes, however, did not shift. Old Tom might as well have been talking to a log. He released Uncle Nigel's hand and stood, staring away over the bog. Then he tipped back his head and gave a long, mournful howl.

Candace reached for the hand Old Tom had just dropped. Uncle Nigel's hand was warm, alive, but when she gave it a squeeze, her uncle failed to respond. "It's as if his mind were a thousand miles away," she whispered mournfully.

Rumblegut stared down at Uncle Nigel. "Aye," he said, nodding slowly. "Or his soul."

"What did you just say?" Kenneth asked sharply.

Candace sighed. "Please, Kenneth," she begged. "Don't be starting another argument."

"I'm not," her brother said. "I just want to know why Rumblegut thinks Uncle Nigel's soul is far away."

Candace turned to the troll. "Do you really think that Uncle Nigel's soul has already departed from his body, even though it's not yet sunset?"

Rumblegut shook his head. "Thine uncle has nae become a will o' the wisp. His body be alive, yet." He shrugged. "But as tae why he dinnae speak or move, 'tis a mystery I dinnae know the answer tae."

"I know what's happened," Kenneth said.

Candace turned, wondering what bit of nonsense he was about to spout now. "What?" she asked belligerently. She swept a hand to include Rumblegut and Old Tom. "Enlighten us."

Kenneth pointed back at the shore with Uncle Nigel's walking stick. "It's Uncle Nigel's creature-catching device."

Candace frowned. "What about it?"

"It's captured Uncle Nigel's soul."

Old Tom turned to stare at Kenneth, a cautiously hopeful look on his face. "Go on, Herr Kenneth."

"Earlier, when I flew over it in the dirigible, I felt something," Kenneth explained. "Old Tom felt it, too. A pull, as if the device was trying to take something from us. Uncle Nigel built the device to capture will o' the wisps, and as Rumblegut told us, will o' the wisps are the souls of the dead. I think the device is also capable of pulling out the souls of the living."

Candace shook her head. "But I stood right next to it and didn't feel anything."

"Maybe you have to be above it," Kenneth said. "Perhaps Uncle Nigel clambered on top of it to adjust it, and was accidentally caught in the electrical net."

Candace nodded her head, her eyes bright. "That would explain why the cabinet was leaning over when the peat cutters found it," she said. "And it also explains what happened to Cumberstone."

"Who's Cumberstone?" Kenneth asked.

"You'll meet him, soon enough," Candace said. "He doesn't have a soul right now, either. But I think I know how to give it back to him—and to give Uncle Nigel his soul back, as well."

Kenneth watched anxiously as Candace grasped the crank on the side of Uncle Nigel's creature-catching device. Rumblegut held the cabinet at an angle to the ground, his massive arms wrapped around its base. The red-headed peat cutter stood a short distance from it, staring blankly out across the bog. Uncle Nigel was off to one side, Old Tom firmly gripping his arm so he didn't stray from that spot. The sparrow's nest had been placed on the ground, well away from where anyone would tread on it.

"Is everyone ready?" Candace asked.

"*Ja,*" Old Tom said.

"Aye, lass," Rumblegut urged.

"Ready," Kenneth answered. "But perhaps I should be the one who—"

"I'm quite capable of turning a crank, thank you very much," Candace said in a frosty voice. "It doesn't take a *boy* to do that."

Kenneth held up his hands. "Go ahead," he said. "I'll just watch."

Candace took a deep breath. "Here we go, then."

She turned the crank.

The tiny crackles of lightning dancing atop the antenna shrank, then disappeared. The sparks flowing into the device seemed to hesitate, then suddenly reversed course. As Candace continued to turn the crank, they flowed up the squared-off coil of wire and exploded into the air with tiny, sizzling pops.

Kenneth frowned, suddenly thinking of something. "There's two souls inside the device," he said. He jerked a thumb at the red-headed peat cutter. "Uncle Nigel's and this fellow's. How do you know which will come out first?"

Candace hesitated in her cranking for only an instant. Then her look of resolve returned. "Why, they should come out in the reverse order that they went in," she said. She glanced at the troll. "Isn't that right, Rumblegut?"

The troll shrugged. "I suppose."

"Careful," Kenneth cautioned the troll. "You're shifting the cabinet."

Rumblegut steadied it.

"We'll know in another moment if I'm right," Candace said. She kept turning until the crank thudded home. The sparks crackled fiercely now; the antenna became hot and started to glow coal-red. Something was forming inside the pyramid-shaped wire; something that glowed. A tiny ball of light the size of a pea.

"His soul!" Candace cried.

With a loud pop that filled the air with a burning smell, the tiny ball of light floated out of the antenna. It drifted toward the red-headed peat cutter. Slowly.

Candace had expected it to home in on Cumberstone, but instead it drifted right by him. "Quick!" she shouted at Kenneth. "Push him into it!"

Kenneth sprang forward and gave the peat cutter a shove. Cumberstone staggered like a drunken man into the ball of light. It hung against his chest for a moment, like a softly glowing burr stuck to his shirt. Then it melted into him and disappeared.

Cumberstone gasped. Twitched. Grimaced.

"Did it work?" Candace asked.

Kenneth shook his head. "I'm not sure. Something doesn't seem quite right. He seems—"

Cumberstone suddenly flung out both arms and flopped face-down on the ground. Twitching, his arms bouncing up and down and legs kicking, he opened and closed his mouth.

Kenneth looked down at him in horror. "What's happening to him?"

Candace shook her head mutely. "I . . . I don't know."

Old Tom looked equally horrified. "You must have been mistaken, *fraulein*," he told Candace. "The device does not function as you thought."

"It must," Candace said. "It has to."

Rumblegut lurched the cabinet upright, let go of it, then dropped to his knees and started scrabbling about. "Yon dragonfly!" he shouted. "Find it, lass."

Kenneth gaped at the troll. He glanced back and forth between it and the flopping and twitching Cumberstone. "What, has the troll gone mad too?"

Candace smacked a hand against her forehead. "Of course!" she said. She, too, dropped to her hands and knees.

Kenneth looked at Old Tom, hoping he, at least, had some idea of what was going on. But Old Tom mutely shook his head.

Candace jumped to her feet, holding something. "Found it!"

"Well done, lass," Rumblegut said.

Kenneth spread his hands. "Could someone please tell me just what in blazes is going on?"

"Kenneth!" Candace said, sternly. "Language." She handed him the dragonfly and pointed to a spot on the ground. "Put this little fellow over there, would you?"

Kenneth stared down at the bug in his hand. The dragonfly sat meekly on his palm, wings limp. Not moving. Just like Uncle Nigel. Kenneth glanced at the twitching, bulging-eyed Cumberstone. Understanding suddenly dawned. "A dragonfly's spirit?" he asked incredulously. "Inside Cumberstone's body?"

Candace nodded. "Quickly now," she said. "Before Mister Cumberstone injures himself."

Kenneth jumped to it. He set the dragonfly down on the ground, then backed rapidly away. Rumblegut, meanwhile, wrapped his arms around the cabinet and pointed the antenna at Cumberstone. Candace turned the crank.

Lightning danced atop the antenna, sparks crackled—and a tiny ball of light materialized amid Cumberstone's red locks, then detached itself from his scalp and drifted back to the cabinet. As it drifted toward the antenna's coil, Rumblegut shifted the cabinet so that it pointed at the dragonfly. Candace reversed the crank and sent the ball of light drifting away from the cabinet once more. This time, it moved through the air in a tight spiral, directly toward the spot where the bright blue insect lay. It landed on the dragonfly's back and was absorbed into it. A moment later the dragonfly fluttered its wings and flew away.

Candace heaved a sigh of relief. "Right," she said. "Now on to Cumberstone."

She started to direct Rumblegut to point the cabinet at the peat cutter, but Kenneth caught her arm. "What if it's Uncle Nigel's soul that comes out next?" he asked, worried. "Or another dragonfly?"

"Not to worry," Candace said. "You saw how the dragonfly's soul headed straight for it. We'll know which soul comes out next by the direction it naturally wants to follow. We'll place Uncle Nigel and Cumberstone side by side, and let the soul choose its own course."

They did as she suggested, Kenneth standing Cumberstone up while Old Tom walked Uncle Nigel to a spot a few steps away from the peat cutter. Then Rumblegut swung the cabinet back around so the antenna was pointed midway between them and Kenneth backed away. Candace turned the crank again and a new flow of sparks began. This time, the glowing ball of light that manifested inside the antenna was much larger, the size of a tennis ball. When it detached from the device, it spiraled toward Cumberstone.

Kenneth watched, fascinated, as the ball of light struck the peat cutter's chest and dissolved into his body. An instant later Cumberstone shook his head. He glanced down at the mud that covered the front of his trousers and shirt, made a half-hearted effort to brush it away, then squinted around at the others. "Has Master Owen been found yet? Is he here to give me my pay?"

Candace smiled. "That's Cumberstone, all right."

As a second tennis-ball–sized sphere of light materialized inside the antenna, Kenneth grinned. "Uncle Nigel will be here in a moment," he told Cumberstone.

The peat cutter nodded.

Kenneth watched as another ball of light detached itself from the antenna. Would it spiral toward Uncle Nigel—or was it the soul of yet another creature that had been caught in the device? Kenneth held his breath, waiting. He saw that his sister was doing the same. They shared a hopeful look.

Old Tom released Uncle Nigel's arm and stepped back. The ball of light headed directly for Uncle Nigel. It settled against his broad chest, flattened, was absorbed . . .

"Uh!" Uncle Nigel folded over, as if shot. One hand shot out, scrabbling in the air, as if desperately trying to grip something. Then he straightened.

He looked at Kenneth and blinked several times, as if not seeing him properly. Looked at Candace, whose hand was on the crank. At the troll, who was holding the cabinet. At Old Tom, who had taken Uncle Nigel's elbow again to steady him.

Uncle Nigel looked confused. "Where did you lot come from?"

Kenneth whooped and held his hands in the air like a boxer celebrating a victory.

Candace let out a deep, heartfelt sigh of relief. "You were trapped inside the device," she said. "It pulled out your soul."

Uncle Nigel frowned. "It did?" He reached into his pocket and pulled out a soggy handkerchief to wipe his brow, noticed it was filthy with bog water, and tucked it away again. "I see," he said, staring at the cabinet. "Funny, it seems only a moment ago that I was taking photographs of the will o' the wisps. Just as they were drawing close to shore, I noticed the cabinet start to topple to one side, and hurried back to catch it as it fell. The last thing I remember is pushing it upright. That must have been when it happened."

Uncle Nigel took his walking stick from Kenneth and gave a faint laugh. "Imagine—a creature catcher, getting caught by his own device." He took a deep breath, visibly composing himself. "Thank you, children, for freeing me. I might have been trapped inside that cabinet for a very long time."

"Who's that talking?" Cumberstone asked. "Master Owen?" He glanced above him, squinting at a cloud.

"Ah, yes. I see the dirigible now. I'd best get about my work, then." He stumbled away, arms extended, feeling for a mooring line that wasn't there.

Uncle Nigel clapped a hand around Old Tom's shoulder. "Not one of the better men you've hired, is he, Thomas?" Then, seemingly fully recovered now, he strode toward the cabinet, which was humming and sparking. It wasn't producing any more balls of light, though. Uncle Nigel's soul—and those of Cumberstone and the dragonfly—seemed to have been the only things it had captured.

Uncle Nigel shaded his eyes with a hand and peered at the spot where the sun was sinking below the horizon. "Ah," he said. "It's dawn, I see." He pointed at Rumblegut. "You there. Troll. Be a good chap and point that thing out toward the bog, would you? There may yet be some will o' the wisps hanging about. If there are, I mean to catch them."

"Oh, aye?" Rumblegut's eyes narrowed. One of his hands shifted toward the crank. Slowly, he began to turn it in the other direction.

"Rumblegut, no!" Candace cried, catching his arm.

Kenneth was dumbfounded. Uncle Nigel had only just gotten his soul released from the device. His uncle's speedy recovery didn't surprise Kenneth, but his single-mindedness did. "After all that's happened, you still want to chase after will o' the wisps?" Kenneth sputtered. "Why, if it hadn't been for Candace and me—"

"Yes, indeed," Uncle Nigel said. Distractedly. Like Kenneth's father. "Well done. A fine rescue, indeed."

179

"If it weren't for us, you would have died at the bottom of the bog," Kenneth continued. "And it isn't dawn—the sun's setting, not rising. You've been underwater an entire day. After your soul was caught, the will o' the wisps led you out to a deep spot, and your body sank like a stone."

"Really?" Uncle Nigel glanced down at his clothes, which were soaking wet. "Underwater, you say? For an entire day?" He sounded as though he didn't believe Kenneth. "How could that be possible?"

"Magic," Rumblegut said firmly.

"You were in the bog, all right," Kenneth added. "Six feet under. Drowned—or nearly so. If it weren't for the fact that the cabinet had already stolen your soul, it would have risen out of the bog to become a will o' the wisp, had we not found you before sunset. That's how will o' the wisps are made. They're souls, risen from the dead." Kenneth shook his head. "You said you knew all about will o' the wisps, but I'll bet you didn't read a single book about them, did you?"

Uncle Nigel threw up his hands. "Read a book!" he cried. "Now you're sounding like your father. It's not as though you'll find will o' the wisps in the pages of some dusty old mythologica. They've not been studied before. And there wasn't time to go poking about in a stack of books. If I'd spent too much time dithering about, Eberts or Higthorn might have beaten me to the punch. No, by all that's mighty, I may have experienced a little setback, but I'm going to be the first to capture a will o' the wisp."

"And do what with it, exactly?" Candace interjected. "Put it in a zoo? It's someone's *soul*."

Uncle Nigel frowned down at her. "Why, Candace Owen. Don't tell me you're siding with your brother on this point."

Candace nodded her head. Firmly, as Mother would do. Arms folded against her chest, she turned to the troll. "Rumblegut—that cabinet. Destroy it."

"Aye, lass. With pleasure." Holding the cabinet in one arm, Rumblegut balled his other hand into a fist. One punch, and the cabinet splintered. Another, and its internal components shattered and began to smoke.

"No!" Uncle Nigel cried. He tried to rush forward, but Old Tom held him back. "Herr Owen, it is dangerous. It stole your soul."

Uncle Nigel watched, wincing each time Rumblegut's fist descended. "But with a few adjustments . . . it might yet . . ."

Rumblegut finished smashing the cabinet. He yanked the wires out of the top of it, then hoisted the cabinet, which was sparking furiously, over his head. Then he heaved it out into the bog. It landed with a loud splash.

Uncle Nigel's face fell as he watched it sink. For a moment, Kenneth felt sorry for him. But Uncle Nigel recovered his composure quickly. He turned, his shoulders square.

"Well then, children," he said. "That's that." He glanced at his camera. "At least I managed to obtain some photographs of the will o' the wisps. Let's get back to the dirigible, and make our way home."

Kenneth stared at the ground. "About the dirigible, Uncle Nigel. It, ah—"

Old Tom stepped forward. "What your nephew is trying to tell you, Herr Owen, is that the dirigible is no more. We used it to search for you. Unfortunately, Herr Owen, it crashed."

Uncle Nigel raised an eyebrow. "Crashed?" He closed his eyes for a moment, then sighed. "It seems it's more than just a camera I'll be replacing, this time," he said. Then he forced a chuckle. "You children are getting rather expensive."

He turned to Old Tom. "How did the crash happen?"

"The pixies caused it, Herr Owen."

Uncle Nigel's other eyebrow rose. "Pixies?" he asked, incredulous.

"It's rather a long story, Uncle Nigel," Candace said, limping forward. "The pixies captured me, and then they captured Kenneth, but Rumblegut—"

"Rumble . . . who?" Uncle Nigel asked.

"Oh, that's right," Candace said. "I forgot to introduce you. Uncle Nigel, meet Rumblegut."

The troll extended a massive hand to Uncle Nigel and cocked an eyebrow, as if daring their uncle to test his grip.

Uncle Nigel returned the troll's smile. And his handshake. He winced—only a little—as the troll squeezed his hand. "Pleased to meet you, Rumblegut," Uncle Nigel said. At the same time, he leaned, slightly, in Kenneth's direction. "Well done, lad. I've not seen a finer specimen."

Rumblegut's eyes narrowed.

With a start, Kenneth realized his uncle thought that he had captured the troll. "You're mistaken, Uncle," Kenneth whispered back, glancing nervously up at the troll. "I didn't—"

"Me spuggies!" Rumblegut suddenly roared. Flinging Uncle Nigel's hand aside, he charged away with great, pounding strides that shook the ground.

Startled, Kenneth peered in that direction. Cumberstone was fumbling about near where the troll was running to; perhaps he'd mistakenly trodden on the nest. The peat cutter turned, squinting in alarm, as Rumblegut bore down on him. The troll, however, merely knocked the peat cutter aside and dove for something on the ground. Something that stood next to the nest: a small, green-skinned man in soggy, mouse-fur trousers and vest, holding a fledgling sparrow whose neck he was about to wring.

The same pixie who had plunged the knife into the dirigible's gasbag.

Roaring with anger, Rumblegut lifted the pixie into the air. "Why, thee . . . thee scaumy little—" The pixie dropped the sparrow at once. Carefully, gently, Rumblegut lifted the fledgling from the ground and placed it back in the nest. Then he stared at the squirming pixie, his glassy eyes bulging. "As for ye, pixie, I've a mind tae—"

"Don't kill him!" Kenneth said.

Rumblegut gave him a puzzled look. "After all the grief these hae put thee through, lad, I'd hae thought thee happy tae see yon pixie crushed."

Kenneth smiled. "I have something else in mind for it."

"Oh, aye?" Rumblegut asked. "And what would that be?"

"You'll see."

Candace, meanwhile, was staring out at the bog. She tugged on Kenneth's sleeve, then silently pointed. Glancing in that direction, Kenneth saw bright balls of bone-white light rising from the water, out over the spot where Uncle Nigel had been submerged.

Will o' the wisps. And they were starting to drift this way.

Uncle Nigel spotted them, as well. He stared at them a long moment, then turned and picked up his camera and tripod. "Children," he said, "we'd best be moving away from here, before those will o' the wisps get any closer, or we'll all wind up drowned, this time."

11

Candace and Kenneth followed their parents into the auditorium, which was rapidly filling with members of the Royal Cryptozoological Society. Most were men—hearty-looking individuals who had probably seen as much adventure as Uncle Nigel had—but a handful were women. As she took her seat, Candace spotted Gertrude Bell, the "daughter of the desert" who had studied the flame creatures of Persia, and Mary Kingsley, who had brought back, from darkest Africa, a snakelike fish called the nyamiyami that could double the volume of any water it was placed into. Unfortunately, this fact was only discovered after one of the main halls of the British Museum flooded.

Uncle Nigel stood on stage behind the podium, ready to deliver his lecture. He smiled broadly at Candace and Kenneth, and nodded at their mother and father. He had fully recovered since their return by coach to London two weeks ago; his skin was its usual sun-bronzed color.

As the audience settled themselves on their chairs

and gradually hushed, Uncle Nigel gestured at someone who stood just off stage. Old Tom emerged from behind a curtain, carrying a slide lantern. He set it on the stage, then struck a match and touched it to the lantern's mantle. A soft glow shone through the lens. Old Tom waved out the match, then left the stage and took a seat near the back of the room. Uncle Nigel inserted the first glass slide as the lights in the lecture hall dimmed.

"I should like to present to the members of the Royal Cryptozoological Society an illustrated lecture on my most recent expedition," Uncle Nigel began. "An expedition to the Moorlands to capture a will o' the wisp."

Polite applause followed.

The first slide showed a rectangle of black against a starry sky: the cabinet, set up at the edge of the bog. Uncle Nigel told the audience what the cabinet was, and explained that he had designed it to catch will o' the wisps. "That, however, was something I later chose not to do," he added.

"Chose?" Candace said under her breath.

"I don't think he wants to tell anyone about . . . what happened," Kenneth whispered back.

More slides followed. These showed will o' the wisps rising out of the bog in the distance. Uncle Nigel talked about how will o' the wisps lured people into deep water. Their victims, he said, did not drown, but entered a state of "magical suspension" that ended at sunset with their deaths.

As the lecture progressed, the audience fell into a

rapt silence. Soon they were leaning forward, hanging on his every word.

The final slide showed a close-up view of a glowing ball of light, inside which were dark shadows that looked like eyes and an open mouth.

"As will be evident from this final slide, the will o' the wisp is, in fact, not swamp gas but the non-corporeal remains of those who drown in the bog," Uncle Nigel told them. "A living *soul*."

The audience murmured and shifted uncomfortably on their chairs.

"Which is why," Uncle Nigel continued, "I decided not to use my device, but to destroy it. For just as it is a crime to dig up the bodies of the dead, it should likewise be a crime to collect their souls."

In the thoughtful silence that followed, more than one head nodded.

"Hear, hear," one man said.

"Bravely done," another called out.

Uncle Nigel smiled, then stroked his mustache. "I also learned, during my expedition, that it is not just humans whose souls are so fiendishly ensnared by will o' the wisps. A will o' the wisp does not limit itself to capturing humans—it will also seek out other creatures with souls. Trolls, for example, or—"

A man sitting behind Kenneth snorted. "You can't mean to say that *creatures* have souls," he protested aloud. "They have an animating spirit, I'll grant you, but not a true soul."

Kenneth's mother twisted around in her seat to confront him. "Of course they do," she hissed. "That's why it's so important that—"

"Indeed they do," Uncle Nigel said before she could finish. He glanced down at the twins, and gave them a wink. "Even the lowly dragonfly has a soul—albeit a tiny one."

There were more mutters of disbelief at that.

"I propose," Uncle Nigel continued, "a new classification system for cryptozoological creatures. A revolutionary new system that would divide them into two broad categories: creatures that are equal to humans, in terms of both intelligence and emotion, and creatures that are mere beasts. I propose that these be named *Creatura intellexi* and *Creatura bestia*. I put it to the society that the latter—creatures equivalent to animals—may indeed be captured and kept as specimens. The former, however—intelligent creatures, like trolls—should not be captured or caged, but left to their natural habitats, for they are the equals of men."

A hubbub of voices that filled the room. Some sounded excited, others outraged.

"And women," Mother called out over the general noise.

"And, of course, women," Uncle Nigel added, bowing slightly to her.

He straightened and signaled for the gaslights to be turned up again. "That concludes my lecture," he said. "Except to tell you about the paper I'll be writing for the next issue of the *Cryptozoological Journal.* It will be an astounding case study of a classic *Creatura intellexi*. The werewolf."

"I didn't hear anything about him capturing a were-wolf," a man behind Kenneth murmured to the catcher sitting next to him.

"Perhaps he means to study the one in the Berlin zoo," the other man answered.

As Old Tom came forward to remove the slide lantern from the stage, Kenneth caught his eye. Old Tom nodded slightly, then smiled.

"Old Tom must have told Uncle Nigel he's a were-wolf," Candace whispered into Kenneth's ear.

Kenneth nodded, glad to hear that Old Tom had taken his advice.

There was no time to talk further about it, however. Uncle Nigel was patting the air, gesturing for silence. When the confusion of voices finally died down, he motioned for Candace and Kenneth to rise.

"And now, for our second feature of the evening," he said. "Ladies and gentlemen, I present to you my niece and nephew, Candace and Kenneth Owen, who accompanied me on my latest expedition and who will now present their own findings."

Polite applause filled the room once more as Candace and Kenneth walked up onto the stage. Candace was ready to deliver her talk, but she was nervous. So was Kenneth, by the look of him. He waved her forward. "Ladies first," he whispered.

Candace took a deep breath and stepped up to the podium. As Uncle Nigel took a seat in the front row next to Father, she stared out over the audience. Father sat perched on the edge of his seat, his book forgotten on the floor beside him. Mother sat next to him, smiling. She was wearing a bright red sash that read, "Suffrage for All" in block letters. She'd made sure that everyone in the audience saw it as she came in late to take her seat, but for once Candace didn't mind. Society women didn't attend the lectures given by the Royal Cryptozoological Society; they were too busy taking tea with the right sort of people or cutting ribbons at garden openings.

But even if Lady Agnes Hawthorne herself had been in attendance, Candace wouldn't have cared. The time for fretting about the feelings of others was long past. Candace was a woman of action, now, like Bell or Kingsley. And she had a message to impart.

She shuffled her lecture notes. The sheets of paper felt damp in her hands. "Contrary to popular belief," she began, "trolls do not eat children, nor do they turn to stone in sunlight. They do, however, experience periods of hibernation, particularly after eating protein-rich soils, like those with a high earthworm content. During these prolonged rests, they resemble a boulder or other, static part of the landscape, to the extent that birds will sometimes build nests on their broad shoulders.

"But most surprising of all," she continued, "is the troll's enormous capacity for compassion. Not only will trolls go out of their way to rescue a child in distress, they will resist the urge to harm a smaller creature that has annoyed them—even though their anger can be a fierce thing, indeed. Trolls are every bit as intelligent and sentimental as human beings, and as such, they deserve our respect. They are equally as deserving of their freedom as any man—or woman—present."

"Hear, hear!" a woman's voice cried out stridently. Candace didn't need to look up to know that it was her mother's. Candace gave a slight smile, then continued.

"And with that, I present my entry for the *Londinium Times*' contest. Not a creature I have captured, but a creature who has captured my heart. The troll named Rumblegut."

Candace walked to the rear of the stage and tugged on a braided pull cord. Curtains parted, revealing a grinning Rumblegut, who had been waiting silently all this time. He raised his arms and roared, stomping forward across the stage with heavy footsteps that all but splintered its boards. A number of the creature catchers recoiled, and one or two even leaped to their feet.

"Look out!" one man cried. "He's broken his chains!"

Rumblegut grinned widely, his crystal teeth reflecting the yellow gaslight that lit the stage. Then he bowed, as elegantly as any gentleman.

Candace nodded toward a dour-faced, elderly man with white hair and a drooping white mustache who was seated in the front row, then winked at Rumblegut. On cue, the troll turned to the explorer and extended a hand. "Doctor Livingstone, I presume?"

Delighted chuckles filled the room.

Livingstone rose to his feet with the aid of a cane. He extended a hand—one that trembled, slightly, from the malaria that had plagued him during his explorations of Africa—and shook the troll's hand. "Rumblegut," he said in a voice that was firm, despite his advanced age. "Delighted to meet you."

The audience broke into wild applause.

As Livingstone resumed his seat, Rumblegut turned and offered Candace his arm. She took it, and together they moved to the side of the stage where the photographer from the *Times* had set up his tripod. He was the same fellow that Candace had crashed into at the zoo.

"No roller skates this time?" he quipped. "That should make things easier. And less expensive." He advised Candace and Rumblegut to stand very still, adjusted his camera, then touched a match to the magnesium powder in his tray, setting off a bright white flash that sent a thick cloud of white smoke billowing toward the ceiling.

When the photographer was done, Rumblegut stepped down from the stage. An usher tried to steer him to the back of the room, but the troll ignored his gestures and settled on the chair in the front row where Candace had been seated. The chair groaned under his weight, then shattered. Rumblegut's bottom thudded to the floor. He shrugged, then grinned. The people behind him leaned to the other side, trying to peer around him, as Kenneth walked to the rear of the stage and lifted a cloth-covered object from the table it had been sitting on. Kenneth placed this atop the podium, then struck a pose, hands on hips.

"Pixies," Kenneth told the audience, "are not the beautiful, gentle creatures described in children's books. Not at all. They are cunning as a medusa, slippery as a Tartarian eel and fierce as a rakshasa demon. They can appear harmless at first glance, but are capable of ensnaring an unwary passerby with something as innocent as a dance. Follow a pixie in a circle, and you are trapped within its mushroom ring forever. Unless," he added with a smirk, "you are handy with a stone and can smash that mushroom ring even while dancing like a whirling dervish."

He paused, taking in the looks the members of the Royal Cryptozoological Society were giving him. So far, they were merely nodding; Kenneth hadn't told them anything they didn't already know from the lectures that Eberts and Higthorn had given, several years earlier. But the best was yet to come.

Kenneth turned and removed the cloth from the large jar on the podium. Inside the glass was the pixie that Rumblegut had captured. It stared fiercely out through the glass at Kenneth with evil yellow eyes, then squeaked an oath at him and shook its fist.

Kenneth pulled a tin from his pocket, opened it, and took out of it a sliver of raw beef. He forced the chunk of meat in through one of the holes in the jar lid. "Pixies," he told the audience, "eat meat."

As if on cue, the hungry pixie pounced on the sliver of beef and stuffed it into its mouth. Blood trickled down its chin. "More!" it squeaked.

Kenneth set the empty tin down beside the pixie's jar and turned back to the audience. "It is popularly believed that pixies subsist entirely on the meat of small birds and rodents," he told them. "It is also believed that they trick humans into dancing with them out of a sense of loneliness, or as an amusing diversion. But their purpose is far more sinister. The truth is—" He paused to hike up his trouser leg, revealing bandages on his ankle and his calf: one over the wound the pixies had inflicted with the pocketknife, the other over the nasty bite the one on the dirigible had given him. "The truth is that pixies eat human flesh. Like the fierce piranha fish found in the rivers of South America, they gang up on their victims and take them down. One bite at a time."

A murmur swept through the audience. Several of the men leaned forward to eye the bandages, then muttered knowingly and touched a hand to their own, more ancient, wounds. Kenneth expected to see his father pulling uneasily at his collar, or perhaps going pale, but his expression was as fiercely proud as Uncle Nigel's. And just a little envious.

Kenneth realized, in that moment, that perhaps his father wished he could have adventures, too.

He reached into his pocket for the second item he'd

brought. "After careful research," he said, a word that got an approving nod from his father, "I have learned the one weakness that all pixies share: a fascination for intricate patterns." Not yet revealing what he held in his hand, he picked up the jar and unscrewed the lid, loosening it. The pixie watched, grinning slyly. When Kenneth opened the lid, it bent down in a crouch, ready to leap out. Before it could, however, Kenneth stuffed in a piece of lace. The pixie glared at it, glanced away, looked back at the lace again—then picked it up and sat cross-legged on the floor of the jar, staring intently at it.

Kenneth didn't bother to replace the lid. "Show a pixie a piece of intricate lace," he told the audience, "and the pixie will stare at it for hours, completely enraptured. It is a puzzle a pixie simply cannot put down. Yes, a simple lace-trimmed handkerchief is the perfect object—if you don't have a troll handy—with which to capture a pixie."

The audience broke into applause. Kenneth bowed, then reached into the jar and carefully removed the now docile pixie. He crossed to the side of the stage where the photographer waited, and posed, presenting the pixie triumphantly on his palm. Then he moved to where Candace and Rumblegut stood.

"Nicely done," Candace whispered.

"And you, as well," Kenneth replied. He smiled at Rumblegut, then added, "Both of you."

A man who had been seated at the side of the stage rose to his feet and approached the podium. He

motioned for Candace and Kenneth—and Rumblegut—to approach. He was a tall man, but round in the middle, with a softness that came from years of sitting at a newspaper desk. His hair had receded until it was little more than a fringe over his ears. He bowed as Kenneth and Candace approached, then turned to the audience. As the publisher spoke, Kenneth slipped the pixie—still fiercely clutching the scrap of lace—back into its jar and screwed on the lid. No sense taking chances.

"Ladies and gentlemen of the Royal Cryptozoological Society," the publisher announced, "I present to you the winners of the *Londinium Times* creature-catching contest for children. The first place is a tie, between Candace and Kenneth Owen."

More applause followed. Kenneth heard a man's voice shout, "Bravo!" and saw that it was their father. He'd actually risen to his feet and was applauding wildly, as if one of his hounds had just won a race. Beside him, Uncle Nigel thumped his walking stick on the floor. He had a wide grin on his face—so wide it crinkled the scar on his cheek.

The publisher turned and presented first Candace, then Kenneth, with a copy of *A Child's History of England*. Candace curtsied and thanked him, then nudged Kenneth with her elbow. Kenneth was inclined to elbow her back, and sharply, too—he didn't need any reminders about being polite—then sighed. Same old Candace.

"Thank you, sir," he told the publisher as he tucked

the book under one arm. "I shall treasure this always." He already had plans, however, to trade the book for something more entertaining. A pellet gun, perhaps.

The publisher was about to usher Kenneth and Candace from the stage when Uncle Nigel abruptly stood. Tucking his walking stick under one arm, he strode onto the stage. "A moment, if you please," he told the publisher. He pulled a small jewelry case from his pocket and opened it. A silver medal was nested on each side of its velvet-lined interior. Kenneth gasped as he recognized the two matching medals: each was a Victoria Medal for conspicuous merit in the advancement of cryptozoology.

Uncle Nigel handed one of the medals to Candace, another to Kenneth. He motioned for them to put the medals on. They did, slipping the medals' ribbons around their necks and grinning widely. Uncle Nigel smiled, then turned them to face the audience.

"Ladies and gentlemen, I present to you the newest—and youngest—members of the Royal Cryptozoological Society: Candace and Kenneth Owen. They have proved themselves creature catchers of the highest order, not only by returning to Londinium with such outstanding specimens, but—"

"Specimens?" Rumblegut growled from the front row.

"Such fine specimens of trollhood," Uncle Nigel smoothly continued. "And, ah, pixiehood."

The audience applauded again. Rumblegut stood, and took a bow.

As the ceremony wound down and the twins stepped off the stage, Candace nudged Kenneth—but not hard. She seemed to just want his attention. "Now that we've won the contest, what are you going to do with your pixie?"

Kenneth shrugged. "Show it to the boys at school, I guess. Then—" He noticed that Rumblegut was standing close by, listening. "Then set it free, I suppose. Maybe in the Underground. It can help keep down the rats." He tilted his head in Rumblegut's direction and lowered his voice. "What about . . . him?"

"It's all been arranged," Candace said. "Rumblegut's going to stay on for a while, here in Londinium. Mother's arranged for him to go on a speaking tour. After that, well, I'm hoping to persuade Father to hire him as our gardener."

"Aye," Rumblegut said, "I'd like that."

Kenneth grinned at his sister. "Do you suppose we can persuade Uncle Nigel to take us along on his next expedition?"

Candace returned his smile. "Blackmail him to, more like. If he doesn't, we'll tell everyone what really happened, out there on the moors." She paused. "But why not set out on our own expedition, just you and I? I've decided to collect plants, rather than creatures. Perhaps a Hindu gem tree, or a Sumatran destiny tree. They say that, if you pick the leaves off, you can read your destiny just like reading a palm. Or perhaps a Chinese pantao, which grows a single peach of immortality every three thousand years."

Kenneth shrugged. "Sounds like a long time to wait. And where's the excitement in going and digging up a tree?"

Candace's eyes gleamed. "Ah, that's where you're wrong. The pantao tree is guarded by a mated pair of fu dogs, which are every bit as fierce as lions—and magical, as well."

Kenneth grinned. "Fiercer than Mrs. Soames's little beast?"

Candace nodded.

Kenneth stuck out his hand. "Count me in," he said. They shook hands.

Kenneth smiled. He and Candace wouldn't be setting off for China anytime soon, but when they did manage to get there, they'd go together.